IN THEIR FATHER'S COUNTRY

Anne-Marie Drosso

In Their Father's Country

TELEGRAM

ISBN: 978-1-84659-059-7

Manufactured in Lebanon

TELEGRAM
26 Westbourne Grove, London W2 5RH
Tabet Building, Mneimneh Street, Hamra, Beirut
www.telegrambooks.com

1924: Selim

In the late afternoon of November 19, 1924, while Cairo nervously awaited the British response to the downtown shooting of Sir Lee Stack, Sirdar of the Egyptian army and Governor General of the Sudan, bedridden Selim Sahli was thinking of another shooting.

In 1921, during the Alexandria street riots over the British presence in Egypt, a policeman had killed a man watching the melee from a balcony. The victim's family – Greek working class – had launched a lawsuit. The case had worked its way up to the mixed court of appeal, and was scheduled to be heard at the end of the month. An experienced lawyer, Selim accepted the case *pro bono*. He had already prepared his argument that the court's reach extended to the policeman's action for no arm of government should be above the rule of law. It would be a hard case to win, which made him all the keener to have a go at it. His head propped up by pillows of assorted sizes, he wondered whether he would have the strength, come the end of the month, to address the court.

Until the previous evening, he had assumed that he would. Now, after an especially difficult night and a heavy dose of painkillers, he felt almost as weak as he had in Paris after his last kidney operation. Reluctant to pass the file to his partner Mahmud Bey, who had two difficult cases of his own to argue, he decided to give himself another forty-eight hours before calling him. In the meantime, Selim would polish his submissions. The sight of the files stacked high on his bedside table invigorated him. Yet a shooting pain in his back stopped him from reaching for them. Losing heart, he remembered with exasperation Nietzsche portraying illness as a state conducive to fruitful contemplation. 'Rubbish,' he thought.

The curtains of his bedroom window were drawn back and the shutters pulled up. The windows themselves were opened just an inch, as he liked to hear the sounds of the city and feel connected to the hustle and bustle of the outside world. It kept his spirits up.

With its thick Persian rugs, Venetian lamps, canopy bed and walnut furniture, his bedroom bore all the signs of affluence. Yet, compared to other bourgeois Cairene bedrooms at that time, it was almost austere, lacking the usual profusion of ornamental objects. Though decorative, alabaster bookends on a small writing desk, and silver jewelry boxes on a dressing table served a utilitarian purpose. The fine white gauze curtains were not shiny satin; the one mirror in the room had a reddish oak frame with a matt finish, rather than a gilded frame. Black and white lithographs – mostly street scenes – covered half of one wall, while three large overfilled bookcases took up the entirety of another.

The apartment was within walking distance of Groppi's, the Café Riche, Lemonia's, the Muhammad Ali Club and Au Bouquiniste Oriental, all places Selim frequented but had not set foot in since the worsening of his kidney condition over two weeks ago.

A couple of minutes passed before the pain in his back diminished. Small as it was, this improvement made him euphoric and he thought again about his case until his two daughters, fifteen-year-old Gabrielle and fourteen-year-old Claire, came rushing into his room.

Gabrielle burst out loudly in French, the language she spoke with her parents: 'Papa, Sir Lee Stack has been shot.'

'Really?' Selim asked, sitting up in his bed. 'Really?'

'Yes, yes. At lunchtime. In his car. On his way home from the war office, I think. Apparently, a group of young men standing on a kerb shot at his car as it slowed in traffic. His driver and aide-de-camp were hurt too. The three of them have been taken to the Anglo-American hospital,' Gabrielle said, her voice rising in excitement.

'Well, well ... ' Selim said. 'I must call Mahmud Bey. He might tell us more about it.'

'What do you think this will mean for Egypt's independence?' Claire asked.

'Not much in the long run. Trust me, Britain's so-called special relationship with Egypt won't last long. Egypt will sooner or later achieve total independence. Whether democracy takes root is another question though. Will Saad Zaghlul manage to steer the country in the right direction? Does he have the personality for it? One wonders. There seems to be a bit too much of the autocrat in him.' After a brief pause, Selim went on, 'Did I ever tell you that, years ago, I spent a couple of evenings discussing Rousseau with his brother Fathi who was in the midst of translating *The Social Contract*? Now Fathi Zaghlul had strong liberal instincts, even if he had some lapses – but then no one is free from contradictions. May he rest in peace.'

The two girls exchanged quick glances, taking it as a good sign that their father should be so talkative. He had been unusually subdued the previous evening. Their father's precarious health had been a source of worry for them all their lives. He had sought treatment in Europe summer after summer. By now, they should have been inured to his bouts of illness. But since he rarely took to his bed, they were upset when he did. Their mother, herself very anxious, was incapable of providing the sort of reassurance that would have made the girls worry less about their father's plight.

'Papa,' Claire asked, 'why didn't you ever become involved in politics?' She recalled him supporting the 1919 lawyers' strike and her mother's concern when he took part in demonstrations. But why hadn't he joined a party and become really involved? 'After all,' she said, 'you're for much of what the nationalists are for.'

Plump and balding, Selim had lively hazel eyes with a witty, attentive and kind expression. He put people at ease when he talked to them and made them feel that what they said mattered a great deal; because of this many found him handsome when he was actually quite plain. Even in his debilitated state he managed to look attentive. He took his time before answering.

'The Syrians of Egypt are in an awkward position,' Selim said, 'so are the Greeks, the Lebanese, the Armenians, though we, the Syrians, are probably in the most awkward position. Is it our fault, for wanting to be all things to all people, or the fault of those among the nationalists who blow our distinctness out of proportion? A bit of both, I suppose.'

'Papa, don't tire yourself,' Gabrielle said and looked at her sister disapprovingly.

'Don't worry. I'm feeling fine. It just occurred to me that you two might want to read Rousseau at some stage. It wouldn't be a bad idea.'

'And should we be reading Marx too?' Claire asked. As a student, her father had returned from Paris with the first two volumes of *Das Kapital* in his trunk. His father would not have it in his household and had ordered his son to get rid of the books or not bother unpacking. Selim complied, leaving a note which read: 'No to censorship!' He was taken in by an accommodating aunt who suggested a compromise. Selim could go back home with his *Das Kapital* as long as he kept it out of his father's sight, hidden somewhere in his room, and the father, pressured by his wife, had relented. This was what one of Claire's uncles had told her.

'Marx?' their father said, 'Marx too if you have the inclination. Read everything and anything, despite what the nuns tell you at school.' Without a pause, he added cheerfully, 'I suggest you now do something more useful with your time than keep me company, and I should try to do some work.' Upon seeing his cook walk into the room carrying a tray, he said, 'Ah! Here's Osta Osman bringing me a camomile infusion. But where's my *mehalabeyah*?'

'Drinks first, food second,' Osta Osman said beaming. 'But more importantly, how does our Bey feel this afternoon? Much better it seems, thank God. Certainly better than last night.' A big and bulky Nubian, who guessed he was fifty but was not sure, Osta Osman wore ample *galabeyahs* – always white and impeccably ironed – that made him look majestic. He had worked for Selim's parents for many years and was considered part of the household. Though Middle Eastern dishes were his specialty, he could also cook French, Italian and even some German cuisine. The two other servants in the household – Om Batta, the washerwoman, and young Ali, the cleaner – were in awe of him and marched to his tune.

'I'm upset with you,' Selim said as he took the cup off the tray.

'But why?' Osta Osman asked, not seeming alarmed.

'Because you didn't tell me that the British Sirdar was shot. You must have heard about it soon after it happened.'

'I didn't want to interrupt your afternoon rest, my Bey. I was planning to tell you though. I gather that the young ladies have done that already.'

'Yes, they have. So, what do you think?'

'What can one say ... since the Dinshawai affair, things have gone from bad to worse for the British. It's been almost twenty years but people have long memories. That several villagers were hanged, flogged, sentenced to hard labor for the death of one – only one – British officer after a fight which they, the British officers, caused, will never be forgotten or forgiven. I don't need to tell you, my Bey, about the injustice of this sad story! What about the village women wounded by the British? And the young man beaten to death by them? All Egyptians were furious at the outcome of that trial – Muslims and Copts alike.'

In her heavily accented Arabic – unlike their father, both girls spoke it poorly – Gabrielle turned towards Osta Osman and said, 'You're right. I have a Coptic friend at school who gets very upset at the mention of Dinshawai.'

'So she should,' Osta Osman said. Looking at Selim, he asked, 'What do you think Saad Zaghlul will do now?'

'Well, the British will demand the usual. They'll insist that Egypt forget about the Sudan, abandon any claim on it and withdraw its troops. That's for sure. These demands will obviously be unacceptable to Zaghlul and the Wafd, so he'll resign. Then the king will do his best to get one of his henchmen to be the next prime minister. He might succeed but it won't last. As for those the police will arrest, one can only hope that these poor men will get fair trials.' Selim winced and briefly closed his eyes.

Osta Osman promptly took the cup from him, saying, 'What do we care about politics? It's your health we care about. You have exhausted yourself with all this talk about politics. The doctor told us you needed plenty of rest. You look better today than you did yesterday, but I can tell you're tired. You didn't get much sleep last night.'

'Neither did you,' Selim said, in an appreciative tone. 'There was no need for you to spend the night here. Madame Letitia overreacted. She shouldn't have asked you to stay but you know how wives are.'

'I would have stayed anyway. I intend to spend the night here until you feel absolutely fine.'

'I had better get well soon then, before your wife and children start complaining.'

'They're quite all right without me. All they want is your good health.'

'Your wife is very considerate,' Selim said. He then reached for his files, though he did not open them.

Before leaving the room, Osta Osman said he would return with some *mehalabeyah*.

* * *

When Letitia Sahli, black rings around her eyes, woke her daughters the next day, it was dawn. She told them to come and see their father, saying tersely, 'He's not well. I'll call the doctor although I'm not sure he'll answer. I know he wakes up early but not this early.'

Shivering in their dressing gowns the girls hurried down the hallway, their mother behind them.

Sitting on a stool outside their father's room with a heavy woolen scarf wrapped around his head, Osta Osman looked somber.

The girls tiptoed in.

Ashen-faced, his breathing labored, Selim saw his daughters nearing his bed and protested. 'Mother shouldn't have woken you up. It's not an emergency. I'll be feeling much better as soon as the medicine kicks in.'

He reached first for Gabrielle's hand, then for Claire's. 'My darlings, your mother was right; seeing you I already feel better. It has been a bit rough but I'll soon turn the corner.' He pressed their hands and did look somewhat better. His breathing was easier, and his face had more color. The painkillers were finally having some effect. After a short pause he continued, 'You ought to know though that, while children are indispensable to their parents, it is not the other way around. It's one of those few situations in life where asymmetry makes sense, and is even desirable.'

Not knowing how to respond, the girls kept silent.

'You're much loved and cherished by your uncles and aunt. They'll all be there for you, should – God forbid – something happen to me. As for you, my darlings, I know I can count on you to be good to your mother.'

'Oh Papa, don't say those sorts of things,' Gabrielle cried out, holding back tears.

He pressed her hand. 'Come, come, sweetie. I would be a negligent father if I did not tell you that, whatever happens to me, you have your own lives to live. I'm certain you'll live them fully. Just make sure you don't leave mother entirely to her own devices. You know her tendency is to isolate herself and withdraw.'

When Claire spoke, it was to say, 'Papa, which one of Rousseau's writings should we begin with?'

Her father looked delighted. '*Rêveries du Promeneur Solitaire*,' he suggested.

'Also, should I really try to sit for the *bac*? I'm tempted. Very tempted. I have been wondering whether to tell the nuns at school that I would like to give it a try. I'll need you to talk to them, if they're unwilling to help.'

'But really Claire, now is not the time to saddle Father with this,' Gabrielle said crossly.

'Go for it,' Selim told Claire, 'so you'll be the first girl in Cairo to graduate from a nuns' school with the French baccalaureate.' Then he turned towards Gabrielle and said, 'It's too bad we didn't think of it earlier. It's too late for you to get the ball rolling, but I have no doubts whatsoever that you would have done very well in the *bac*.'

He released their hands and closed his eyes. Every now and then, he would twitch, and one of the girls – by now both were sitting on his bed – would ask, 'Papa, do you need anything?' Each time, he assured them, 'No, no, I'm all right.' For a brief while, he seemed to be dozing; the girls, however, did not dare leave the room. It was he who, with his eyes still closed, urged them to get ready for school. He even encouraged Claire to talk to the head nun about her intention to sit for the *bac*. 'The sooner, the better,' he said.

As the girls got up, they saw their mother, holding a cup and saucer with shaking hands glide, phantom-like, through the room. She looked even more drawn than earlier. With a quick tilt of the head, she motioned for them to go.

The girls hurried out of the room. Osta Osman offered to boil eggs for breakfast.

When the girls returned from school, it was Osta Osman who met them at the door. From the look on his face, they understood.

Their father had died while they were on their way home, just before the doctor was scheduled to pay his second visit of the day. Selim was only fifty-three years old, two years younger than Sir Lee Stack who would die from his wounds a few hours later.

* * *

Selim Sahli's funeral was strictly a family affair, as he had requested. It was held at the Greek Catholic Cathedral of Darb al-Geneina, the first regular Greek Catholic church built in Egypt. Besides Letitia, Gabrielle and Claire, attending the service were his brothers Yussef, Naum and Zaki accompanied by their wives and children and his sister Warda with her daughters. His youngest brother Naguib was in Paris. Osta Osman also attended the service.

The residential center of the Greek Catholics of Cairo for much of the nineteenth century, Darb al-Geneina was the neighborhood in which Selim's forefathers had set up house upon entering Muhammad Ali's service as high-ranking administrative officials soon after their arrival from Syria in 1810. There, they had established themselves in grand quarters. The cathedral was built on land they had ceded.

On their way to the Greek Catholic cemetery in old Cairo, Warda – a buxom forty-year-old with a fickle husband whose frequent overseas travel she only nominally deplored – dissolved into tears. Sitting opposite her in his big Buick, her brother Yussef noted that it was the first time in a long time he had seen her shed genuine tears. Of her five brothers, Selim, the oldest, had been the one most willing to listen to Warda talk endlessly about her real and imaginary troubles.

Selim's death had stunned his brothers and sister. They had grown accustomed to seeing him recover after each illness. When he was told over the telephone by his brother Zaki that Selim had died, Yussef's immediate reaction was to shout, 'But how? I was just about to call him to ask for some legal advice.'

Yussef was shaken by his older brother's death. Even though they had had their disagreements, Yussef was deeply attached to him. Selim curbed his money-grabbing impulses. In his early forties, already rich beyond his expectations, Yussef realized that he would miss his older brother's sobering influence. His own instinct was to grab opportunities without worrying too much about their legal or moral aspects. It was over ten years now since Yussef had concluded a deal – knowing full well that Selim would take a dim view of it – that backfired and threatened to land him in jail. The court case had been long, complicated and nerve-wracking. He had been very frightened, though he had admitted this to nobody, not even to Selim who, at the expense of his law practice, devoted most of a year to the case, and managed, in the end, to get him out of a very tight corner. Yussef felt enormously indebted to him.

While patting Warda's hand – she was still crying – he thought of their mother. She had died before judgement in the case had been rendered. Some relatives had said at the time that the trial had killed her, which had filled him with guilt. Selim's death revived those guilt feelings. Selim had been their mother's favorite. Yussef had no doubts that his death would have destroyed her.

'If Selim were still with us, he would tell us what to expect now that the British have issued their ultimatum to parliament,' Warda managed. Removing his hand from hers, Yussef exclaimed heatedly,

'Really Warda, what a thing to be thinking of. Think instead of how Letitia, Gabrielle and Claire must be feeling. Besides, since when are you so interested in politics?'

The morning after the funeral, dwarfed by the huge armchair in which she took refuge – Selim Sahli's armchair – Letitia Sahli announced to her daughters, with a quavering voice but dry eyes, that she could not endure the thought of receiving condolence visits. Their uncles and aunts would have to receive the visits in their own homes. Small and dainty, she had just turned forty. With a vacant stare – her abundant auburn hair pulled in a severe bun and her face free from any trace of make-up – she explained to the two bewildered girls that she could not imagine herself hearing platitudes about the death of their father. Without him, she said, her life threatened to become as barren and desolate as the Egyptian desert; a country in which she still felt, even after all these years, so terribly alone.

Of their mother's background and family, the girls knew nothing other than that she was Italian and that she had been, in her youth, an accomplished rider. They had discovered this by chance, after coming upon an old riding outfit of hers at the bottom of a trunk, whip and boots included. The outfit had to be hers for the boots were unusually small and the trousers' waist almost a child's size. She had unusually small feet and a waist that could be encircled, almost in its entirety, with two hands. Teased about their discovery, she had conceded, without divulging more, that she had ridden on a regular basis when she was younger. Her silence about her past was so all-encompassing and her reluctance to break it so palpable that they had never dared probe. Claire had asked her father just once why she had no family on her mother's side. He had answered that it was a private and painful subject for her mother, that people were entitled to keep silent about hurtful subjects, and that she would be better off thinking of all the relatives she had, on his side, as opposed to those she did not have, on her mother's side.

'I only have you two now,' Letitia said to her daughters.

'Mother, this country is our country. Father's country. You cannot refuse to receive condolence visits. You cannot,' Gabrielle cried out.

'Gabrielle, I'm suffering enough as it is. You want to make things even harder for me?' The mother looked in her daughter's direction without seeming to see her.

Gabrielle's voice acquired a frenzied tone, 'But the presidents of both bar associations will be coming to pay their respects. Uncle Yussef said so. Even the president of the Chamber of Deputies might come, despite his busy schedule. Father was much loved, both in the mixed courts and in the native courts. Think of him! You cannot close the door in people's faces.'

Letitia looked down and said nothing.

'Mother, say something,' Gabrielle insisted, moving closer.

'I told you that those visits would be unbearable for me. Unbearable,' Letitia said.

'But why? Why?' Gabrielle repeated, towering above her mother with all her height. Turning towards her sister, she demanded, 'Claire, talk to Mother, talk to her,' after which she ran out of the room shouting, 'What will people say? What will people think?'

Her heart racing – Gabrielle's explosive temper still dismayed her, though she should have grown used to it – Claire stood still. Standing in one corner of the room, all she could think of was, 'But what's to become of us now?' while telling herself that it was her father's death and not her future that she should be thinking of. Yet the more she tried to focus on the death of her father, the more it was her life that seemed to matter.

Her mother too was still, with that faraway look that tended to invite belligerence on Gabrielle's part and solicitude on Claire's.

Banging noises came from Gabrielle's room, at the other end of the apartment.

'Don't worry, Mother,' Claire said, rushing towards her. 'Don't worry, you know how Gabrielle is,' and she put her hand on her mother's shoulder.

'Only you understand me,' her mother said.

'Gabrielle loves you. She does,' Claire said.

'Go talk to her, console her,' said Letitia. 'You remember her tantrum over the birthday dress? You were barely six years old. She was terribly upset, and Papa told you to go cheer her up? Remember?'

'Yes, I do,' Claire said. How could she not? It had all started at lunchtime with Gabrielle, a seven-year-old girl already conscious of her looks, declaring, 'I will not go to Lola's birthday party wearing the dress I wore at Mona's party. I need another dress!' When told by both her father and her mother that she would have to resign herself to wearing the same dress, she had chanted, 'I don't want to, I don't want to.' Her father had then said, with utmost calm, 'All right, you'll get your new dress; tomorrow we'll walk past Uncle Yussef's office, and you'll trade your dress for the dress worn by the little girl who sits by the building selling jasmine with her mother. You can wear that dress to Lola's birthday party.'

Screaming, 'No, no, no,' Gabrielle had got up, without asking to be excused, and had dashed out of the room, followed by Osta Osman begging her to finish her lunch.

'But poor Gabrielle,' Claire had tried to intercede on her sister's behalf, terrified at the prospect of her sister being actually forced to wear the tattered dress worn by the little jasmine-seller. Never having heard her father issue any threats, she feared he meant business.

'Poor?' her father asked. 'Hardly. You must learn to use words more judiciously, Claire. The little girl who sells jasmine is poor, but Gabrielle is not. Though I suppose your sister is in need of consolation. So you go to her, and do your best to cheer her up. Tell her I love her, that she's still my darling, that you both are.'

Thanks to a small lie, Claire had succeeded in comforting her sister, telling her that, at Mona's birthday party, she had heard two girls say that they found her dress so pretty they wanted one just like it. Getting the dress out of her wardrobe, Gabrielle had judged it to be special enough to warrant being worn to another birthday party.

'Please, go talk to Gabrielle now,' Letitia urged Claire.

* * *

About to knock on Gabrielle's door, Claire recoiled upon hearing her lament, 'Why did it have to be him? Why him?' She quickly looked behind her to ensure that her mother was nowhere near, retreated to the end of the hallway, and closed the door to the living room. Then she took refuge in her bedroom, where she sat at her desk and rested her head on its cold surface. The emotion she had – perhaps wrongly – attributed to her sister was lurking in her own heart too. 'Forgive me, Mother,' she whispered and tried to suppress her sobs.

While Claire and Gabrielle were giving vent to their anguish

– grieving alone in their bedrooms – their mother wept in the privacy of hers.

It was the thought that her father would deplore their being divided in mourning that eventually drove Claire to get up, compose herself and go see her sister. She found Gabrielle sitting at her desk, with a collection of postcards – from Paris, Vittel, Ostend, Lyons, Venice, all places her father had gone to for his cures – spread out on top.

Gabrielle quickly gathered the postcards and stuffed them in a big envelope. 'So, has Mother come around?' she asked Claire with a sullen air, as if she expected the answer to be negative. 'If she sticks to her decision, I intend to talk to Uncle Yussef.'

'But let her be. She's free to do as she pleases,' Claire said and immediately regretted her confrontational tone.

'But it's a matter that concerns us too! Besides, you know her. Left to do as she pleases, she would never go out, never socialize. Have you already forgotten how much Father used to have to prod her?'

'He knew how to handle her.'

'We cannot let her isolate herself. He said so himself.'

'It seems to me that this is a different issue,' Claire began, then pleaded with her sister, 'Gabrielle, I beg you not to harass her about it. Please.'

'Will we always have to walk on thin ice with her? Make special allowances?' asked Gabrielle. 'Respect wishes that have no rhyme or reason?' She was now pacing up and down her bedroom.

'Black suits her,' Claire observed, but fearing that her sister would find the compliment ill-timed, she kept that thought to herself. 'I have been meaning to tell you that Father believed you would make a great lawyer,' she said instead.

'He never said so to me,' Gabrielle said, coming to a stop, then she asked, with incredulity in her voice, 'When did he say that? When?'

'Last week. He told me that you had all the aptitudes needed to study law, and you could easily get accepted into the law faculty on the strength of your school record, without the *bac*.'

Gabrielle's face lit up and she sat on her bed, saying, 'It pleases me to hear that. It really does. Why don't you sit down, Claire?'

Shoulder against shoulder, the two sisters – for that brief moment full of love for one another – let their thoughts about their future take an optimistic turn.

* * *

Later that day, Claire would raise with her mother the subject of the duel her father had apparently fought some ten years earlier. She had overheard, at the funeral, her Aunt Warda make mention of it and being rebuked by her brother Yussef for it. 'Selim had his unpredictable side. Who would have thought that he would fight a duel? He of all people,' Warda had said.

The image of her mild-mannered, rational father fighting a duel naturally grabbed Claire's imagination, its chivalrous side appealing to her. Yet at the same time, it seemed unthinkable to her that he should actually have done so. And like most children faced with unexpected revelations about their parents, she was troubled.

Alone with her mother in her father's study, Claire adopted a light tone to ask, 'Well, Mother, tell me about Papa's duel.'

Her mother glanced in her direction. 'Papa's duel?'

'Yes, Mother. Papa's duel,' Claire said gently.

'Who told you about it?'

'A little bird,' Claire said. Then she revealed, 'I heard Aunt Warda mention it.'

'You know that I like your aunt a great deal, but she talks too much. She would have been in her element in the theater; your father was right.'

'Mother, what about the duel? When did it take place, and why?'

'Oh! It would have been in 1912 or 1913 ... I'm not quite sure anymore. Why? Because men easily take umbrage. That's why.'

'But he was not a hot-headed sort.'

'He had his moments.'

'What exactly happened?'

'Claire, it's all in the past. One of his colleagues made a remark which your father found unacceptable. They were in the chambers of the mixed tribunals. One thing led to another. The duel took place a couple of days later – a duel by sword. After a few rounds, your father was wounded in his forearm and the attending doctors declared that the injury put him at such a disadvantage that further rounds were out of the question. He and his colleague made up on the spot.'

'If doctors were present, there must have been witnesses too.'

'Yes, there were.'

'It must have been a real duel then?'

'Yes! Yes!'

'I'm amazed. Are there any documents concerning it?'

'I'm not sure and, in any case, I have no idea where they would be. It was not such an important thing, Claire. Really.'

'But how did it all start?'

'I already told you. One of Father's colleagues made an

objectionable remark. Papa asked him to withdraw it, he didn't, so Papa slapped him. That's what led to the duel.'

'At the time the duel was fought, Gabrielle and I were very little. Didn't he think he was taking some risks?'

'You don't think things through in the heat of the moment.'

'I would love to see any documents about it,' Claire told her mother in a pressing though still gentle way.

'If I find any, I'll show them to you, but, please, don't tell Gabrielle. It might needlessly agitate her.'

'I won't. Where was the duel fought?'

Suddenly more relaxed, her mother flashed a smile and said, 'Not far from the Mena House Hotel. In the shadow of the Pyramids.'

* * *

That same night Claire had a nightmare in which her father lay bleeding on a dune, sword in hand, surrounded by his whole family looking on helplessly. Claire woke up with a start, hearing herself scream, 'Papa.'

Jumping out of bed, she threw her dressing gown loosely over her shoulders and, barefoot, ran to her father's study, where she began hunting for any document that might tell her more about the duel.

She found none, though she rummaged through each one of the desk drawers.

It was past one o'clock in the morning. To keep warm, she slipped on her dressing gown and tied its belt tightly around her waist. Still sitting at her father's desk, she tried to picture him at the time he fought the duel. In his early forties, he would have been more athletic-looking, though on second thoughts perhaps not. In her earliest childhood memories, he was already rotund. A skilled swordsman? It hardly seemed possible. Probably a bad swordsman, even if willing to fight. What did she know about him and what didn't she know? Loving of her mother but not always faithful to her. She knew that. He had had at least one affair – with a Swiss milliner who lived in Alexandria. Again, it was her Aunt Warda who had let that slip in front of her. Her mother, however, had never manifested any knowledge of that affair, or of any other. Had his extended stays in Europe been really only health-related? Had he, at times, too easily accepted her mother's withdrawn character, using it as an excuse to go out on his own? And why hadn't he – a man so sympathetic to Egyptian nationalist aspirations – insisted that she and Gabrielle learn Arabic properly? And what had been his true feelings about his brother Yussef? Why had her father gone so much out of his way to extricate her Uncle Yussef from the big legal morass he was in that one time? Simple brotherly loyalty? To shield the family from disgrace? Because it had made him feel good to be so much needed by his successful young brother? Now that her father was gone she would never have answers.

Exhausted, though reluctant to go to bed, Claire heard a faint noise, like soft steps gliding over tiles. She held her breath and thought she saw a silhouette hurrying past the door to the study, which she had left open. Her head buried in her lap, she whispered, 'Papa, wherever you are, protect me. Protect us. You must.' Then, all was quiet again. But Claire remained glued to her chair until she heard the hallway clock strike twice.

Forcing herself to be brave, she quietly rose from her chair and hurried out of the study. In the hallway, she noticed a ray of light coming from under the closed kitchen door and heard her mother cough. The fleeting silhouette had been neither a burglar nor her imagination.

'Mother,' Claire said, opening the kitchen door.

'I could not sleep so I decided to have a cup of coffee. You know how coffee helps me go to sleep. It always does. I don't know why. But darling, why are you up? Thinking of Papa?'

'Yes, I was,' Claire said and sat at the kitchen table, next to her mother whose long, thick, wavy hair, hanging loose on her back, gave her a youthful appearance. Letitia was more graceful than beautiful. Her looks invited a protective impulse in those around her. Gabrielle seemed to be the exception.

Claire looked tenderly at her mother.

'Claire, there's something I need to tell you. I was going to talk to you about it tomorrow ... to you and to Gabrielle. I might as well tell you now. Uncle Yussef is putting an apartment in one of his buildings at our disposal – the building where he has his office. It's a very nice building with spacious apartments. We'll still be in the heart of town, and we'll be close to him, if we need anything.' Letitia spoke without looking at Claire, her face resting on her slender fingers, her eyes pensive.

Claire had not expected this at all. She objected, 'But we're close to his office anyway. We don't need to move, Mother. Walking to his office takes less than ten minutes.'

Frowning, her mother explained, 'We lived very comfortably on Papa's earnings. More than comfortably. But the situation has changed, darling. We must be careful with money now.' Then she hurried to add, 'But your lives – yours and Gabrielle's – will not really be affected. Besides, Uncle Yussef thinks we ought to move, that it's not such a good idea to live surrounded by memories.'

'Uncle Yussef, Uncle Yussef, Uncle Yussef … but what about you, Mother? What do you want? What do you think?'

'Claire, it's not like you to be difficult. Don't you think we can trust your Uncle Yussef?'

'But that's not the point,' Claire argued. 'We can trust him, but do we want to become dependent on him? I certainly don't.'

'Claire, it was Papa's wish that Uncle Yussef should step into his shoes. After all, he did give a year of his life to get Uncle Yussef out of his legal troubles.'

'Papa's wish?' Claire blurted out, reddening, which was a sign she was getting upset. 'Papa's wish? You're sure? You're not just saying so to appease me?'

'Claire, believe me. He left very specific instructions.'

Claire's heart sank. For the first time in her life she was flooded with negative thoughts about her father. It seemed so obvious to her that Uncle Yussef was the last man to whom her father should have entrusted them. He had not raised them to end up under the thumb of an autocrat, which she knew her uncle to be. In silence, she promised herself that she would chart her own course in life, no matter the Uncle Yussefs of the world.

'How do you think Gabrielle will react to the idea of a move?' her mother asked Claire, giving her a look that begged for reassurance.

'I don't think she'll mind that much,' Claire said curtly. 'I suspect that she'll find the proximity to Uncle Yussef agreeable.' The one good thing about the move, Claire decided, was that her Uncle Yussef might act as a buffer between her mother and Gabrielle, relieving her of that responsibility.

'I can tell that you're angry, Claire. Please, don't be. I need your support.'

'Let's go to bed, Mother,' Claire said. 'Let me put you to bed.

Did I tell you that when you got up tonight and went to the kitchen, I mistook you for a burglar or a mouse?'

'Frankly, I'm more afraid of mice than of burglars,' her mother said, then asked, 'You're sure that Gabrielle will not get upset when she hears about the move?'

'I'm positive,' Claire asserted more confidently than she actually felt. 'But you should probably have Uncle Yussef broach the subject with her.'

Seeming relieved, her mother agreed, 'Yes, it's probably a good idea to have Uncle Yussef speak to her.'

By the time she reached her bedroom, Claire had made up her mind to sit for the *bac*.

As though in need of examining the person she was becoming, the first thing Claire did on entering her room was to open her wardrobe and look at herself in the mirror. She knew that her schoolmates considered her the most beautiful girl in her class. She disagreed. She found her type of beauty a touch insipid. Her classmate Sophie epitomized her ideal of feminine beauty with her dark eyebrows, thick eyelashes, dimpled round cheeks, lively eyes, full lips, an upturned nose, straight jet-black hair and willowy build. Claire's own eyebrows were finely arched, her green-speckled, honey-colored eyes dreamy, her chestnut hair wavy, her face perfectly oval and her nose – the feature she liked best about her face – small and straight. Her shoulders she did not like at all; she found them insufficiently defined. Yet clothes hung well on her. She was a good height – tall but not too tall – and slim. While examining herself in the mirror, she wondered whether her father, whose predilection for petite women was well known, considered her pretty. Her anger at him lingered. That he had given Uncle Yussef such an important role to play in their lives was still incomprehensible.

In bed, it took a while for Claire to find sleep. She speculated on how her uncle would react to her decision to sit for the *bac*. She feared he would object. He was not the kind of man who set a high value on studies for girls, nor boys for that matter. Business and money seemed to be his only interests. Osta Osman was on her mind too. What would happen to him, if they were going to have to live on a tight budget? They could probably still afford Om Batta and young Ali, but Osta Osman? Her Uncle Yussef might want to retain his services – he and his wife entertained a lot. Osta Osman was no fan of her Uncle Yussef, a bossy employer. When her grandmother, no longer in need of his services, had asked Osta Osman whether he would work for either Selim or Yussef, he apparently had answered, 'Selim Bey anytime, but Yussef Bey, if you don't mind my saying so, never.' Claire caught herself relishing the prospect of her uncle making an offer to Osta Osman only to be told by the proud cook, 'Thanks, but no thanks.' But would Osta Osman actually say no to her uncle, whose offer would undoubtedly be lucrative? Probably not, she concluded and yet, until she finally fell asleep, she fantasized about Osta Osman rebuffing her uncle.

* * *

Her face glowing with pride, papers in hand, Gabrielle was standing by the apartment's entrance door. She was waiting for Claire, held up at school with a drawing project.

It was December first, Saad Zaghlul had resigned and Ahmad Ziwar, generally perceived to be the king's man, was called upon to form the new government. How Ziwar Pasha would govern with Zaghlul's Wafd still being the leading party in the Chamber of Deputies was unclear. Would he ask the king to dissolve the Chamber and hold new elections? The king would be eager to oblige since he was counting on a newly formed royalist party to win seats.

Gabrielle's interest in politics blossomed immediately after her father's death. She began reading the papers assiduously. That habit of hers, to a large extent born out of a desire to identify with her father, soon became pleasurable in its own right.

The reason she was so pleased that afternoon had little to do with current political events and the fact that her father had predicted Zaghlul's resignation. It had to do with a eulogy about her father and an obituary.

The eulogy, pronounced before the mixed courts, was by a prominent Cairene lawyer, and the rather long obituary, published in *La Bourse Egyptienne*, by a prominent journalist.

As soon as Claire stepped into the apartment, Gabrielle – eyes shining – said loudly, while brandishing the papers in her hand, 'Claire, you must read this. It's about Papa.'

'Give me a minute. I'm very thirsty,' Claire said, though she quickly glanced at the two texts.

Gabrielle followed her sister into the kitchen, where, after Claire had poured herself some lemonade, the two girls sat on a wooden bench.

Claire looked at the eulogy first. It referred to her father's sober eloquence, his photographic memory, his passion for the law, his ability to get to the core of complex issues as well as to reveal the complexities behind seemingly straightforward questions, his professional probity and his willingness to advance costs out of his own pocket.

'So what do you think?' Gabrielle asked, eager to hear her sister's reaction. 'If only Papa could read this!'

Claire nodded. 'Yes, it's nicely written,' she said and handed the paper back to Gabrielle.

'Is that all you have to say?' Gabrielle asked, surprised and reproachful.

'Well, it's a eulogy and so meant to be full of praise. No?'

'Are you suggesting that it's overstated?'

'I would like it better if it had a more personal touch. That's all.'

Gabrielle scowled. 'Sometimes, I don't understand your reactions,' she told Claire. 'There's no denying that Papa had admirable qualities.'

'I am not denying it at all. Now let me look at the obituary,' Claire said in a conciliatory tone.

Looking displeased, Gabrielle gave her the obituary.

It dwelt on Selim's ongoing health problems, his numerous operations (seven), his stoicism, his equanimity in the face of pain, and the restraint with which he would allude to his health problems the rare times he did. It depicted him as generous to a fault, as a man who had used his powerful intellect to defend not only important causes but also individuals in need.

The last paragraph in the obituary caught Claire's attention. Mention was made of the pleasure Selim Sahli would get from spending time at home with his beloved children and his books after his long, arduous workdays. Yet no mention was made of his wife, their mother. None.

'What's the matter? You seem surprised,' Gabrielle said.

Another rapid glance at the obituary confirmed to Claire that their mother had been left out of it.

'So, what's the matter?' Gabrielle asked again.

'Nothing, nothing!' Claire replied, trying to sort out her jumbled thoughts. Should she or should she not point out the omission to her sister? Surely, Gabrielle must have noticed. How could she have failed to? She must think it was of no consequence or perhaps did not want to talk about it. 'I was thinking of Papa,' Claire said.

'Ah!'

'That's all. Did Mother read the obituary?'

'Well of course! Both the obituary and the eulogy.'

'What did she have to say?'

'She got misty-eyed. She almost cried.'

'But she said nothing?'

'She said, "He actually was pretty much the way they describe him."'

While Gabrielle was re-reading the eulogy, Claire was trying to put her mind at rest. The absence of any reference to her mother in the obituary might be an error, nothing else. But that did not seem an altogether satisfactory explanation. She could not help but ask herself whether there had been more to her mother's refusal to receive condolence visits than the reasons she had given. On that score, Letitia had not budged, and condolence visits had been received at Uncle Yussef's.

It was almost five o'clock, when Osta Osman walked into the kitchen to prepare dinner.

The first thing he told the two girls was that he had heard about the eulogy and the obituary. Earlier in the day, their Uncle Zaki had dropped by to see their mother and had translated the two pieces for him, almost word for word. 'I miss Selim Bey so much,' he said to Gabrielle and Claire. 'Not a day goes by without my thinking of him.'

The doorbell rang. Gabrielle raced out of the kitchen. Claire stayed behind.

'How about some *mehalabeyah* tonight?' Osta Osman suggested. 'With orange water and cinnamon just the way Selim Bey used to like it.'

'That would be nice,' Claire said.

'Don't let sad thoughts weigh on you, you're too young for that. Sad thoughts are for old people like myself. Selim Bey wouldn't want you to be sad.'

Claire smiled and looked at Osta Osman, whose presence was enormously comforting to her. If only she could bury her head deep in his wide chest and forget about the obituary and all her crazy notions.

She could hear Uncle Yussef's booming voice. Combined with Gabrielle's, the two voices jarred on her. Yussef had come to break the news of their impending move to Gabrielle. Her mother had told Claire, first thing in the morning, that he would be coming for that purpose. 'Osta Osman, do you know about the move?' she asked hesitantly.

Osta Osman nodded. 'Yes,' he said while watching the milk come to the boil. 'I heard about it.'

'I wish we could stay here,' she said.

'The apartments in Uncle Yussef's building are very nice,' Osta Osman said and poured the milk into a glass bowl.

Claire could hear Uncle Yussef and Gabrielle talking right outside the kitchen but she did not move.

Osta Osman now stood with his back to the kitchen door. He began peeling potatoes.

'So that's where you are.' With Gabrielle behind him, Uncle

Yussef walked into the kitchen, saying at the top of his voice, 'Why in the kitchen, pretty girl?'

Claire got up to give her uncle a hug, then waited for him to acknowledge Osta Osman. When he finally did, it was with a gruff, 'How are things, Osta Osman?' Then, with his usual imperiousness, he told her, 'Come, I need to talk to you and Gabrielle,' and affectionately patted her cheek.

Without thinking, she said, 'I'll be with you in a minute. Osta Osman was about to show me how to prepare the dressing for the potato salad. We'll be quick.'

Not hiding her astonishment, Gabrielle asked, with raised eyebrows, 'Since when are you interested in cooking?'

Uncle Yussef laughed weakly and said, 'Let her learn. It might come in handy.' To Claire he said sternly, 'Don't be long. By the way, you and Gabrielle ought to spend more time with your cousins. Bella now reads and, believe it or not, Iris does too, even though she's not yet three. She's quite a phenomenon, this little girl.'

As her uncle was leaving the kitchen, two thoughts crossed Claire's mind: that life without her father was now beginning in earnest, and that she and her uncle no longer quite belonged to the same world.

'Don't worry,' she heard Osta Osman tell her. 'Everything will work out. Things always have a way of sorting themselves out.'

'I must go,' she told him apologetically, without asking him how he thought things might work out for him.

1941: Guy

Dear Iris,

Maybe you already know. News from Egypt has a way of traveling fast to Lebanon. Guy died. He died, a week ago, in a motorcycling accident. A senseless accident, on the way from Ismailiya to Port Said, on a Sunday afternoon. He ran into a truck trying to avoid a lone donkey that was right in the middle of the road.

I have been telling myself over and over again that it might not have happened had we still been seeing each other, had I not forced myself to put an end to a situation that seemed to me untenable, in view of his circumstances and mine. Is it possible, Iris, that, if it were not for this step I took so reluctantly, he would have been spending that Sunday afternoon with me, here in Cairo, as he sometimes did, when the coast was clear? That thought torments me. Did you know that he was about to enlist in the Free French Forces?

To think that in my last letter to him, in which I was trying to explain why it was best for us to stop seeing each other, I scribbled 'Nevermore' at the end. Now I feel that I put a curse on him and invited the accident. How ridiculous of me to have adopted that dramatic tone and used such an expression in that context, when I abhor grandiloquence. Compared to a life, a relationship – any relationship – weighs so little. Life is what matters.

He was extremely fond of you. He was fond of Bella too, but he told me, more than once, that, with you, he had special intellectual affinities. He used to joke that, apart from Gabrielle and me, he did not know two sisters more different in temperament than you and Bella.

In that wretched letter I wrote him, I said that I felt as though I was about to be crushed by some heavy object because I knew I would eventually resign myself to the inevitable and go back to my previous life. It suddenly seemed simpler to renounce youth, freedom, the possibility of adventure, the luxury of being in a position to make choices ... to renounce life in short. And why? Out of cowardice. Because the courage to fight and assert myself was ebbing away. Because my previous life, which seemed a kind of death, was still the easiest solution. Because I was caught in an inextricable mesh of obligations and responsibilities and was riddled with stupid scruples. Because I no longer had faith in myself. Because the part of me seeking to break free from conventionality was evaporating. Pride, self-respect, authenticity were giving way to the numbing mindset that appearances must be kept up even though I was under no illusion whatsoever that people would be fooled! I also said that it was a terrible thing to accept defeat with lucidity, that I did not even have the excuse of blindness. It was not an honest letter – not entirely honest. It reflected only in small measure my state of mind. The essential, it left out. The truth was that I had begun to fear that Guy would end up tiring of our relationship and yet assume, out of a misplaced sense of responsibility, a role he did not wish to assume. You can well imagine that this was the last thing I wanted. It was, however, a likely scenario. My decision to leave Alexandre was strictly mine, but given Guy's nature, he was bound to feel some responsibility. I, on the other hand, wanted him to make the most out of his life and not to be carrying unnecessary baggage. After all, I was thirty and he was twenty-seven. He had his own life to think of – both during and after the war. I had already had my chance at life and messed it up by marrying at eighteen a man I fell for at sixteen, against everybody's better judgement – well, except for my poor mother's. You know that I harbor no ill feelings towards Alexandre. I wish him well, and yes, I probably continue to feel some affection for him, but a gulf separates us. And it is not just a matter of the twenty-two years age gap between us. But let me not go on about that now …

Your father once described me to Uncle Zaki as an unemotional sort – I don't remember in what connection. My behavior around the time of my parting with Guy could have been interpreted in that light. I think that you yourself were a bit surprised by my apparent calm. Yet it is not as though I did not feel torn, as though I did not suffer. Sending Guy that farewell letter caused me much pain. After I stopped seeing him, the thought of Guy living his life to the fullest possible extent provided me with some comfort. Perhaps part of my attachment to him was akin to an older sister's hopes and ambitions for a younger brother. Perhaps I had transferred on to him aspirations that had become unattainable for me.

You may think that I am minimizing the role your father played in my break-up with Guy and reconciliation with Alexandre. I know how upset you were with him for intervening on Alexandre's behalf; how you went out of your way to register your condemnation of the pressure he put on me to get back with Alexandre, he who had so fiercely opposed my marriage ten years earlier. Uncle Yussef never does things in half-measures. First and for years, he adamantly opposed the marriage, then he, as adamantly, opposed the separation. These days, not an hour goes by without him consulting Alexandre on all sorts of matters. Their working relationship is at a real high.

Sure, Uncle Yussef played a role in my break-up with Guy, but I ultimately caved in. He could not have made me do it, unless I had been willing to be swayed.

When Guy was stationed in Morocco last year, he wrote to me of his desire to join the air force. He desperately wanted to fly and had asked his supervisors for a transfer. I was frightened, fearing he would be more at risk flying than as an artillery sergeant. Still, I found myself hoping that he would get his wish. His enthusiasm made one want what he wanted.

To think that it was only just over a year ago that he sent me that letter; only ten months ago, that the three of us were at the Casino des Pigeons.

I was on my way to a lecture on Proust earlier today when the phone rang. I ran to pick it up and Nadia gave me the news. She felt awkward and did not know what tone to

*adopt, knowing, no doubt like everybody else in town, the
ins and outs of my story with Guy. I said little, but my voice
must have betrayed my anguish. After I hung up, I fled the
apartment. Not knowing what to do with myself, I ended up
going to the lecture. I was late and had to sit in the back,
which suited me fine. I wanted to see no one – be seen by no
one. All through the lecture, 'what if' scenarios in which Guy
was still alive ran through my mind.*

*When I returned home, I found a note from Alexan-
dre telling me that he would be tied up for the evening and
would not be home until much later. He was going out with
your father. A business dinner at the Muhammad Ali Club
with some Wafdists. Osta Osman, whom I had not seen in
years, was waiting for me. He used to work for us – I mean
for Mother and Father. You were too young at the time to
remember him. He now lives in Nubia and has come to
Cairo for the birth of a great-grandchild. I like him a lot
but my mind was not on making conversation, so I took
him across the street to visit Mother and Gabrielle, wondering whether I should tell them about Guy. The atmosphere
there was execrable. Gabrielle is beside herself since Nicolas
has been sent to the detention camp for Italians out in the
desert. They were on the verge of announcing their engagement. She is also terribly angry with Alexandre for not doing
enough, in her eyes, to try to get his brother out of the camp.
She is basically angry that it's business as usual for Alexandre but not for Nicolas. She does not believe that Alexandre
was spared only because of his years of government service.
As usual, Mother ends up being the primary recipient of her
anger.*

Given the atmosphere at Mother's place, to tell them about Guy was out of the question. I escaped, leaving Osta Osman there. He immediately sensed that tensions were high and was already trying to defuse them before I reached the door.

As I walked out of the building, Constance walked in, looking very drawn. She was on her way to see Gabrielle. Nicolas's incarceration has been very hard on her. Since her sister's death, she lives for her two brothers. It is difficult to tell which of the two – Alexandre or Nicolas – she is more attached to.

She knew Guy died. I assume Alexandre must know too since they tell each other just about everything. She greeted me by saying that 'she was sorry'. Alluding to last year's events, she said that she wanted me to know that she never judged me. Her well-intentioned words filled me with sorrow. I loved him. I did.

Instead of going back home, I walked around the midan *twice, passing by the museum and, each time, I could hear Guy saying that we Egyptians spend far too little time in it, that our attraction to everything French blinds us to our own treasures. When I decided to sit for the Cambridge certificate of English, he gave me a book to read,* Letters from Egypt *by Lucie Duff Gordon, an Englishwoman who had tuberculosis and chose to live in Luxor because of its warm, dry climate. She died there surrounded by her Egyptian servants and local people; her family was back in England. She felt very connected to the country. Her letters, written in the 1860s, certainly give that impression. Guy was totally taken by her descriptions of Egypt. Also by the woman herself, her courage, her independence of spirit and her ability to observe and assimilate a culture alien to her. I felt envious after reading her correspondence. Envious and culpable. As a foreigner, this woman had managed to get to know an Egypt we hardly know, in large part because of our indifference to it. We are very remiss. But would we be embraced by the locals the way she was? I suspect not. Guy could not fully appreciate the distinction I am trying to draw. Although he spent much of his life in Egypt – as you know his father started working for the Canal Company when Guy was eight – he was French, a Frenchman in Egypt. Lucie Duff Gordon was an Englishwoman in Egypt. And what are we? Viewed with suspicion on all sides. Without anchor. We cannot say 'we're this' or 'we're that'. We have a piece of paper declaring us Egyptians but that's all. We lack legitimacy in quite a fundamental sense. Guy believed that I make far too much out of all this.*

You know what I liked best about being around him? The freedom to say anything that entered my mind. He combined two qualities rarely found in the same person: he knew how to listen and he could make virtually any subject interesting.

After my second round of the midan, *I crossed the Kasr al-Nil Bridge. Except for the city lights, it was pitch dark by then. Did you know that, in Morocco, Guy came to like the* 'ud? *The instrument put him in a sweet melancholy mood, he told me in a letter in which he also extolled the virtues of his simple yet arduous army life in the mountains. He rode, swam in icy waters, and hiked. Flying remained his dream though.*

As that letter of his ran through my mind, I wept. For

Guy and for what might have been, had I been other than who I am.

Write to me about him, please do, anything and everything that goes through your mind! Tell me if you were yourself perhaps a tad bit in love with him; I won't be jealous. Don't embellish though. Just talk to me about the Guy we knew.

I am supposed to meet Anastase tomorrow afternoon at the Shepheard's Hotel but will likely cancel. He is still talking about joining the Greek army. You would like him if you got to know him better. There is a dance tomorrow evening – at Roger S. I won't be going. I intend to spend the day swimming laps. Remember the weekend Guy taught us both to float on our backs?

I hear Alexandre. I must appear calm. I shall not talk to him about Guy. It would not be fair. To either one of them.

Your Claire

My darling Claire,

I have made up my mind: I'm coming home. I want to be with you. To hell with the mountains and the treatment. They don't seem to be doing me much good anyway! I don't give a damn about what my father might have to say about my premature return.

Why Guy? Why so vibrant a man with so much purpose and joie de vivre and not one of those who drag their lives like millstones round their neck?

I will talk to you about Guy, my sweet Claire, but in

person. Right now, I would find it hard. I have been thinking of you as much as of him. Stay the way you are, Claire, never change. Please? My father is an imbecile. He is one of those who mistakes displays of feelings for actual feelings, and reserve for lack of them.

Did I love Guy? Perhaps a bit, because I love you. Most of all, I had enormous respect for his intensity and intelligence.

Claire, my Claire, I am young but feel ancient. Why not me instead of Guy?

I cannot wait to see you.

Most tenderly,
Iris

P.S. Go out, Guy would have wanted you to. Go swimming, riding, dancing. Spend time with Anastase, Roger, Lily, Myriam, Selim and the whole gang. Your friends need you.

1946: Letitia

That September morning, her knees sore and legs swollen, Om Batta, who used to work for Selim and Letitia Sahli and whose daughter Batta was now Claire's maid, moved slowly in her two-room dwelling in Sayidah Zeinab, the district in which she had lived all her life. She was getting ready to catch the tram to go to Midan Ismailiya and visit Claire. Having heard, through Batta, that Madame Letitia was not well, she wanted to drop in on her. The previous night, she had dreamt that Selim Sahli was still alive and insisting that his wife travel with him abroad and that Madame Letitia ended up giving way. Om Batta took that dream to signal that Letitia Sahli's days were numbered so she must not delay her visit. She was also keen to see Claire's little girl, about to turn three, as well as get Claire's impression about Batta's state of mind, now that Batta's husband was thinking of taking a second wife.

'If I were you, I would not venture downtown today,' Om Batta's oldest son muttered. 'There might be demonstrations. If there's trouble in the streets, things could get nasty in the *midan*, as nasty as they did at the English barracks, in February. Mind my words.'

Om Batta threw an angry look at her twenty-three-year-old son, Mahmud, a lanky workman in a shoe repair shop.

'Why aren't you at work?' she asked, her tone clearly censorious. 'I'm not worried about being caught in demonstrations. I don't care what happens to me. It's you I'm worried about. You have friends who will get you into trouble. I know some of them are *Ikhwanis*. They're trying to rope you into their activities.' Raising her voice, Om Batta continued, 'Listen to me, Mahmud, I cannot afford to have you end up in jail. Your younger brother gives me enough headaches. Since he has been working in that no-good *ahwa*, he's spending every piaster he earns, and more, on hashish. In case you don't know, he owes money to all our neighbors. All of them! Are you blind? Can you not see that he is stoned much of the time? How he manages to carry trays and serve coffee is a mystery to me. It's not just a casual habit, it's an addiction that is getting out of control! Instead of roaming the streets, you should be taking care of him.' Beating her breast, Om Batta wailed, 'If only your father was alive, none of this would be happening. Your father was an honest man who kept to himself and wanted no troubles for his family.'

'If you don't want the neighbors to know all of our business, talk, don't scream,' said the young man with suppressed rage, then added defiantly, 'I'm old enough to lead my life as I see fit. The friends you're putting down are honorable men who are doing something for the country.' He paused before asking his mother, caustically, 'Tell me, during the last flu epidemic when you got sick, who arranged for doctors to make rounds in the neighborhood, and for free medicine to be distributed? Do you remember, or do you have a sudden memory lapse?'

Om Batta retorted, 'So, do we have to sing their praises night and day for the few good works they do and ignore all the rest?'

'I cannot believe you're so ungrateful.' The young man sighed, then stated briskly, 'As for Hassan, I'll sort him out. You stay out of it.'

'We'll see ... we'll see ...' Om Batta said, doubtfully. 'I gather the demonstrations are about the same old question – when will the British leave – but why not give the prime minister some time to sort out the problem with them? He is a strong man.'

'We want them to leave now. Now! As for Sidqi, he's certainly strong when it comes to cracking down on people like us. Will he be strong with the British? There's no sign of that.'

'What about the Sudan? I heard you discuss that with your friends last week. What do we care about the Sudan? Why should Egypt be so keen on the Sudan? What good would come out of a union with that country? Let the Sudanese look after their own affairs. We can barely look after ours.'

'Mother, you obviously don't understand these matters.'

Smacking her thigh, Om Batta shouted with derision, 'You, on the other hand, understand everything. Haven't your *Ikhwani* friends taught you the most elementary of lessons: respect for your elderly mother should come before all else?'

'Look, the *Ikhwanis* are not the only ones in the country insisting on immediate British withdrawal and on unity with the Sudan. The Wafdists and the left are asking for the same thing – everyone in the country is,' he said clearly fired up. Then he said, more calmly, 'I must go now. How about you? You're still intending to go out?'

'Why wouldn't I? Demonstrations don't frighten me. If I end up shot by your friends or the police, so be it. It will be God's will.'

'If that's the case, let me meet mine and stop worrying about me. And if you're caught in demonstrations, I will have warned you.'

'If your friends are so admirable, perhaps they can fix your brother,' Om Batta fired at her son as he rushed out of the door, saying hurriedly, 'Pay my respects to Madame Letitia and to Madame Claire too.'

To calm her frayed nerves, Om Batta made herself tea. She boiled it longer than usual; it was almost black by the time she poured it in a glass. 'That should do,' she thought as she sat on the one stool in the room; sitting on the floor had become too difficult for her. Although she would not admit it to him, Mahmud had managed to alarm her with his talk about possible demonstrations. She did not think that he had actually joined the Muslim Brotherhood though she suspected that he was on the verge of joining.

While sipping her tea, in which she had put her usual four spoons of sugar, Om Batta brooded about the recent political events. It had been a rough few months for the country. Even the Sahli family had been affected by the political turmoil. In the summer, the Sidqi government had lashed out against leftist organizations, arresting several Alexandrian Greeks suspected of being communists, including friends of Iris and Bella's husbands. Claire's sister-in-law, Constance, had told Batta who had relayed the information to her mother.

Just as she could see no end to the country's political agitation, Om Batta could see no end to her personal problems: uncontrollable sons and an unhappy daughter.

* * *

'I won't be able to see you today,' Claire said over the phone.

'But it's our last opportunity before I sail to Beirut,' her lover protested.

'Pierre, my mother is unwell. I was up much of the night. This morning, I sent Simone to Constance's place, I did not feel up to looking after both Simone and my mother.'

'I don't mean to pressure you, but could we meet for just half an hour? For a short drive? I hate the thought of leaving without having seen you. I really do.'

Claire ignored the question. 'Are you all packed?' she asked. She hesitated before also asking, 'How is Marie taking your trip? Is she still upset about your going away for three weeks?'

'Oh!' her lover said with annoyance, 'Marie will always find reasons to be upset.'

'Don't you think that you're a bit hard on her?' Claire asked.

He gave a sharp laugh. 'I suppose I am. You're her staunchest defender, you know,' then, in a vehement tone, he said, 'Claire, I would really like to see you today.'

'I'll see what I can do. I'll call you at the office if I manage to free myself. But don't count on it.'

'Call me anyway. I'll miss you,' he said. 'Very much. Oh Claire, if only you and I were free!'

'Pierre, it's pointless to torment yourself.'

'You're so reasonable; there are times when I ask myself whether it's self-possession and level-headedness, or sheer coldness.'

Claire was silent.

'Sorry darling. I did not mean to offend you. But it hurts me when you seem or sound detached.'

She said lightly, 'One should never ask oneself too many questions.' Level-headed? An image flashed through her mind: her banging the dining-room table with her fist so hard as to break the thick sheet of glass on top of it – an outburst occasioned a couple of days earlier by an argument between her husband and her sister over how to deal with her mother. Alexandre had accused Gabrielle of insensitivity, and Gabrielle had painted him as lacking elementary common sense. Torn between the two and tired of her perpetual role as peacekeeper, Claire had ended up banging the table and screaming, 'Enough, *enough*!', which had put an immediate end to the altercation, so taken aback were Alexandre and Gabrielle by her explosion.

'Darling, I hope your mother will be much better by the time I get back,' her lover said.

'I'm not hopeful,' she said, her voice dropping.

'I'll call you tomorrow to find out what the doctor had to say. I'll definitely call you.'

* * *

Claire sat by the phone, wondering whether to go out; not to meet her lover but to fetch, from the Italian consulate, forms she needed in case she traveled with her daughter in the spring. Simone was Italian by birth, like Alexandre. The planned trip was a cruise to Cyprus on which recently married Iris and Anastase would be going. Bella and her husband, Aristote, might be joining them. Claire had tentatively agreed to go along, and Alexandre had raised no objections. But there was the question of who would look after her mother in her absence. Moreover, she was not certain that she could afford it. She had recently come to the conclusion that she needed a job – at least part-time. Alexandre was still working for her Uncle Yussef, but for how much longer? Every day brought new tensions between the two men. Before leaving for work that morning, Alexandre had announced, 'Your uncle is mad, mad, and I'm mad to be working for him.'

For almost two weeks now, her mother had taken to the couch in Claire's living room. Two and a half years earlier, a couple of months after Simone's birth, Letitia had shown up at Claire's door with her poodle, saying that she could no longer bear to live with Gabrielle and Nicolas.

There were two bedrooms in Claire's apartment. Alexandre occupied one, Claire with the baby girl, the other. Claire had offered her mother the bedroom with the baby and to sleep on the couch herself, but her mother had insisted on sleeping in the living room. She needed peace and quiet, she had said. So, the living room had been converted into a quasi-bedroom, becoming, more or less, off-limits for little Simone.

Spending much of her day in that one room, Letitia would smile affectionately at her granddaughter whenever the little girl appeared, teetering, by the living-room door. Letitia would ask to see her dolls and stuffed animals, or talk about her poodle (the dog always by her side until it died) before sinking into a contemplative silence.

Over time, it became increasingly hard for Claire to get her mother to step out of her cocoon. At meal times, Letitia had to be coaxed into joining the rest of the family in the dining room. As for the frequent family gatherings organized by one or the other of her brothers-in-law or her sister-in-law – all occasions at which she would have put in an appearance in the past – she virtually stopped attending them. To try to persuade her to go, Yussef Sahli would resort to histrionics (more than his usual fare), but with less and less effect.

Every now and then, of her own accord, Letitia would go to the movies and, if she liked the movie, she would see it more than once. Constance would sometimes accompany her. They got along well. Letitia was by then in her mid-sixties, Constance in her mid-fifties. To each other, they spoke Italian which Constance, with a good ear for languages, had picked up early on in her life by hearing it spoken in the streets of Cairo.

The catalyst to Letitia moving out of Gabrielle and Nicolas's place and into Claire and Alexandre's was Letitia's new habit of walking out of department stores with trivial items she had no need for, such as a collar trimmed with lace. 'How could you have forgotten to pay for it?' Gabrielle kept asking, only to be met with stubborn silence.

Far from acting as a deterrent, Gabrielle's rebuke seemed to have entrenched Letitia's inexplicable behavior. The few times she went to department stores after that, she pilfered an embroidered handkerchief, ribbons, some silk fabric, and a velvety handbag. Fortunately for her daughters, the shop managers were accommodating. They knew the family and liked Letitia so simply took to sending Claire or Gabrielle bills for the items their mother had 'forgotten to pay for'. They would even allow the items to be returned as long as they were in good condition. Thus, their mother's 'forgetfulness' never became much of an issue for Letitia's daughters other than being the cause of intense private embarrassment and perplexity, for she did not seem to be confused in other ways.

The rare times Letitia went out she dressed with as much care and elegance as ever. Very slight all her life, she had become gaunt in her sixties. Food never seemed to be on her mind.

It was only in the last three months that she had started complaining about her health. All of a sudden, she began mentioning back problems, then some discomfort in the hip area, then more diffuse pain. Two doctors, whom Claire called in quick succession, decided that she had osteoarthritis. Both suggested she was a touch neurasthenic.

Her rare outings became rarer. She seemed to lose interest in going to the movies. Constance, who lunched every day with Alexandre and Claire, found it harder and harder to engage her in conversation. There would be a flicker of a smile on her face whenever Simone ventured close to her room, but she no longer made an effort to talk to the little girl. In Gabrielle's presence, she became very tense, as Gabrielle was forever lecturing her. Her sons-in-law avoided her. They did not know how to behave or what to say in the face of her growing taciturnity.

Every day since Letitia started complaining about her health, Claire made a point of keeping her mother company, sitting in her room for a couple of hours, trying to make conversation. If her mother was particularly uncommunicative, she would read.

'I'm sorry you have to put up with me, Claire. I'm not good company,' Letitia would say.

'Mother, I enjoy spending time this way,' Claire always responded. There was some truth in that. She took pleasure in the opportunity for undisturbed reading and in her mother's – albeit silent – presence. Yet now that Letitia had begun refusing to get out of bed Claire was beginning to find those couple of hours oppressive.

Earlier in the week, the same two doctors, whom she had called three months earlier, concluded that it was a clear case of neurasthenia. Both told Claire that she should not allow her mother to stay in bed all day and cater to her every need, that it would only aggravate her mother's psychological condition and soon cause physical problems. When Claire suggested that her mother might be suffering from some insidious disease (she did not dare say cancer, but that was what she had in mind), the doctors reckoned that it was highly unlikely. 'But what about her weight loss?' Claire asked. Neither doctor saw this as a cause of real concern. 'Women either put on weight, or they lose it after a certain age,' one of the doctors assured her. 'She just happens to fall in the category of those who lose it, which is not a bad thing.'

In spite of the doctors' advice, Claire could not bring herself to force her mother out of bed and into an armchair.

* * *

The ringing phone startled Claire, deep in thought.

'How is she?' Gabrielle asked in her usual abrupt manner.

'Much the same,' Claire said.

'Has she gotten up a bit? Have you managed to have her spend some time in the armchair?'

'No.'

'Tell her to make an effort. You really must.'

'I don't think she's up to it.'

'The doctors think otherwise. It's not up to us to make a diagnosis. Why bother consulting doctors if you're not going to heed what they say?'

'I'm not convinced they're right. Yes, she has depressive tendencies, but she never used to fuss about her health. She never used to complain about being in pain. I don't get the sense that she's playing it up.'

'No one is accusing her of pretending she is in pain,' Gabrielle exclaimed. 'But to stay in bed, all day long, is madness. She needs to move a bit. I bumped into Bella and Aristote in front of Uncle

Yussef's office yesterday. Both said she should make an effort. Aristote should know. He is a surgeon after all. You must get her to sit up every day, you must,' Gabrielle declared categorically. Then, without giving her sister a chance to comment, she said, 'By the way, Cicurel sent us a bill. It seems that, on her last outing, she decided she needed a hat. Didn't you notice her return home with it?'

'I have had other things to worry about than mother's shopping habits'.

'You call these shopping habits?'

'Oh for God's sake, drop the subject,' Claire cried out, then, to her own surprise, she whispered into the phone, 'Gabrielle, I fear she's dying.'

'What on earth are you saying? The doctors are saying nothing of the kind.'

'Perhaps the doctors are wrong.'

Gabrielle was silent for a few seconds then said, 'I'm sure you're dramatizing but we could ask Aristote to recommend some other doctor, if that will provide you with some peace of mind.'

'We should do that. I'll talk to Bella later today. I have to go now. I hear noise in her room.'

'I may drop by in the evening. Nicolas advised me against going downtown during the day. He heard that there might be a big demonstration in the early afternoon. Any sign of it?'

'No, none. I really must go now. See you later then.'

* * *

When Claire opened the door to her mother's room, Letitia was humming in her sleep. Claire was taken aback; never before had she heard her mother hum or sing, even though her Aunt Warda had once hinted that Letitia used to be a singer. The humming was melodic and cheerful.

Curiously, instead of reassuring her, the humming worried Claire. It somehow reinforced her premonition that her mother did not have much longer to live. Studying her mother's hollow face – the hollowness made the nose, never her mother's best feature, protuberant – Claire remembered another one of her Aunt Warda's tales.

'I'm not for you, Monsieur,' her mother was supposed to have told her father when he began courting her, after seeing her slip her tiny feet in the water, in Venice; he, who judged a woman's beauty by the size of her feet and waist, was apparently charmed right away. True, or simply a family tale, reflecting the unspoken feeling in the Sahli family that Selim could have done much, much better than Letitia Graziano, who was sweet, dainty and gentle but had a nebulous background and no standing in Egyptian society?

'I'm not for you, Monsieur': had Letitia been forced by economic circumstances to trade on her charms as many young Italian women, even of middle class background, had had to do between the 1870s and the 1900s? Might she have been a cabaret singer or, a more humdrum possibility, a governess looking after wealthy children on holidays at the Lido, where Selim Sahli apparently first set eyes on her?

Claire suddenly felt the need to know more about her mother.

The humming stopped.

Claire moved next to her mother and whispered, 'Mother, are you alright?'

Letitia opened her eyes, looked bewildered for a moment, then reached for her daughter's cheek and gave it a light stroke. 'Claire,' she said – her voice faint – 'I worry about you.'

This baffled Claire. 'Don't worry about me. I'm fine.'

Her mother went on, 'I sided with you, when you insisted on marrying Alexandre, then sided with you again when you wanted to leave him. I have always wanted for you what you seemed to want for yourself. Was I right?'

It was more than her mother had said in weeks.

'Would you like something to drink?' Claire asked. Her mother's mention of the choices she had made was unsettling.

'Not really, but I'll force myself.'

'I'll go and get you a drink then.'

Her mother's face contracted. 'Oh! I am sore all over, all over.'

'Where exactly, mother? Where?'

'All over.'

'We'll call another doctor. I'll ask Aristote to find us a bone specialist,' Claire said as she held her mother's hand.

Letitia shook her head, insisting that she did not want to see a doctor.

The bell rang.

'It must be Batta back from the market. I'll let her in and get you some juice,' Claire told her mother.

'I'm feeling a bit better. Take your time,' her mother said. She did look slightly more relaxed.

* * *

Om Batta was at the door carrying a big brown bag full of grapes, figs, dates and prickly pears. 'For Madame Letitia,' she said, after hugging and kissing Claire. 'For little Simone, I brought some sweets. But more importantly, tell me how Madame Letitia is doing. When Batta told me that she wouldn't get out of bed, I decided I had to come and see her.'

'I'm glad you did. Perhaps you can persuade her to have a proper meal. But have some tea or coffee first. You'll be shocked to see how much weight she has lost.'

'But she was already skinny. She cannot afford to lose weight. And here I am, putting on weight.'

On their way to the kitchen, Claire noticed that Om Batta was hobbling. 'Your knee?' she asked.

Om Batta laughed, 'My knee, my ankles, my feet, my whole body. I'm old, Claire. Old!'

'Don't say so; you're not old at all,' Claire said, though she was thinking that Om Batta, probably only in her mid-fifties, did look old.

'And where's Batta? Shopping?' Om Batta asked.

'Yes, she should be back anytime.'

'And Ali?'

'Cleaning the windows.'

'Alexandre Bey and *Mazmazel* Constance are well?'

'Yes, they are. Simone is at Mademoiselle Constance's place.'

'I must see that little princess of mine, on my way home I'll drop by *Mazmazel* Constance. Batta told me that Gabrielle's little girl is now walking. How time flies!'

While washing the fruits, Om Batta voiced her concerns about Batta. 'Her husband is saying that he needs children and it's Batta's fault that they have none. He won't even consider the possibility that he might be the problem. I suggested they see a doctor, but he refuses to see one. He won't hear of it.' Her eyes now fixed on Claire, Om Batta said, 'I don't need to tell you about the turmoil a woman goes through when she wants children and none comes. You know all about that. But then, as you also know, sometimes, all of a sudden, by the grace of God, a child is on its way. I have given you as an example to Batta; I told her to be patient and not give up hope. I'm sure it's her husband who cannot have children. I think he senses it, and that's why he refuses to see a doctor. He even does not want her to see one. So, what am I to do?'

'You ought to have her see a doctor without telling him. He doesn't need to know. At least she'll find out whether she can get pregnant. Don't you think so?'

'And what if the doctor says that she's fine? What do we do then?'

'You tell her husband. It might persuade him to see a doctor. He may have a small problem that could be fixed.'

'If only he were that reasonable!'

'It's true, he may never agree to see a doctor,' Claire conceded, recalling how Alexandre had avoided seeing a doctor all the years she was desperately wanting to get pregnant.

'Well, if he's the one with the problem, taking a second wife will not get him children! That should be a consolation for Batta. Unless this second wife of his decides to take the matter in her own hands, if you know what I mean. That's always possible.' Om Batta chuckled.

Changing the subject, Claire asked, 'How are the boys?'

'You mean the men? They're men but behave like boys. I would rather not talk about Hassan. He breaks my heart. He's totally irresponsible.' Lowering her voice, Om Batta said, 'He takes drugs; I'm at my wit's end.'

'Have Mahmud talk to him. You must! Before it's too late,' Claire urged her, 'or Batta's husband could talk to him.'

'No, not Batta's husband! We're best to leave him out of that. He would use it against Batta. I don't trust him. Mahmud, yes; just this morning, I told him to talk to Hassan. But Mahmud has his own drug.'

'What do you mean?'

'He is all taken by the *Ikhwanis*. I know I can confide in you. It's happening under my very eyes. Religion, I am all for! But the *Ikhwanis* frighten me!'

'What does he say about them?'

'He defends them! Mind you, he has a point when he says that they're the only ones in the country who do something for people like us. They're not all bad, though I don't tell him that. I don't want him to think that I favor his joining them. It's too dangerous!'

'You're absolutely right', Claire said, 'he could end up in worse troubles than Hassan.'

'My head spins when I think of all this,' Om Batta said. 'Let me go see Madame Letitia. That's what I came for, not to trouble you with these insoluble problems.'

It occurred to Claire that she could run to the Italian consulate to do her errand while Om Batta kept her mother company. 'Would you mind if I went out for half an hour while you keep Mother company?'

'Of course not, but I'm worried about you going out. What if there are demonstrations? Mahmud thinks there might be trouble in the streets today.'

'Don't worry; I'll be quick. If I see anything out of the ordinary, I'll turn around.'

'Go out then. You need some fresh air. You're as beautiful as ever, but you look tired. And don't you worry about Madame Letitia. I'll look after her.'

When Om Batta walked into Letitia Sahli's room with a glass of freshly squeezed lemon juice, the ailing lady immediately perked up. 'Where have you been?' she asked.

* * *

Driven by the urge to get the forms she needed for that spring cruise, Claire hurried to get to the Italian consulate and back within the hour. The consulate was a mere fifteen-minute walk from her apartment. It occurred to her that Pierre might be calling in her absence and that she would then have to think of some excuse for having gone out without trying to reach him. It also occurred to her that he did not know about the cruise, not yet. 'Oh well!' she thought and decided to put him out of her mind, then immediately felt sorry for him. He was, after all, very much in love with her. It was not his fault she couldn't reciprocate.

While crossing Midan Ismailiya, she looked in the direction of the British barracks to see if there was any sign of trouble. All seemed normal, although the streets were quieter than usual, the trams and buses not quite as crowded. Some people must have decided to stay home.

At the corner of Suleiman Pasha Street and the *midan*, she exchanged greetings with the newspaper vendor. Behind his colorful array of papers and magazines, he was sitting cross-legged on the ground, next to his wife, also cross-legged with a baby on her lap and a toddler by her side. A couple of older children were leaning against her back. Claire nodded to the woman. She had known her since childhood. The little girl selling jasmine in front of the building where Claire's Uncle Yussef had his office was now married to the newspaper vendor and had grown into a large woman with a magnificent smile she flashed at Claire whenever Claire happened to walk by.

At the consulate, Claire did not have to wait to pick up the forms she needed. There was nobody in the waiting room and no queues in the hallways.

The employee who gave her the forms – a cordial young man – was fluent in French and eager to chat. He volunteered that, being married to an Italian, she could apply for Italian citizenship. She had never thought of applying. 'But would it jeopardize my Egyptian citizenship?' she asked. 'It might,' he said, 'but you need not use your Italian passport here. You could use it in Europe.' She said that she would give the matter some thought. While she was gathering her papers, it occurred to her to ask a question that had never entered her mind before. 'Do you keep records on Italian residents living in Egypt?'

'We have records on some, not all. It depends on whether we had dealings with them.'

'I'm wondering whether you have anything on Letitia Sahli? My mother,' Claire asked, half-wishing she hadn't.

The young man looked at her quizzically. 'I'll check. As you can see, I'm not busy this morning.'

'I'm in a bit of a hurry,' Claire said.

'I'll be quick,' he said and winked. 'Take a seat.' He pointed to a chair in the hallway. 'You're also welcome to sit at my desk.'

Claire waited in the hallway, going over, in her mind, the few facts she knew about her mother: her birth date; her maiden name; her parents' names; her time in Venice, if Aunt Warda's story was true; and that she had gone horse-riding at some point in her life – seriously enough to have owned a riding outfit.

When the young man returned, she was not surprised to hear that he had found nothing. She even felt a measure of relief, and yet she found herself asking, 'What about Letitia Graziano? Might you have something under her maiden name?'

'If we have anything, it would probably be under her maiden name,' he said as he disappeared in the back room.

When the young man came back, he was carrying a file. 'I found her,' he declared in a self-satisfied tone. 'Letitia Graziano married to Roberto Goldoni.' He handed the file to Claire, saying, 'I'm sorry but you must look at it in my presence. We cannot let the files out of our sight so why don't you sit at my desk and take your time.'

Claire barely managed to stop herself from blurting out, 'But that is not my Letitia Graziano; it must be another Letitia Graziano,' for even in the state of confusion in which the young man's statement had thrown her, she gathered that it *was* her Letitia Graziano, and that she now held the key to the mystery of the obituary that had so puzzled her at the time of her father's death. A trite and obvious mystery: Letitia Graziano was not Selim Sahli's wife, or their marriage had been irregular in some way.

The first page in the file confirmed to Claire that this Letitia Graziano was her mother: same birth date and same parents.

Claire abruptly closed the thick file and got up.

'You're not going to look at it?' the young man asked, disappointed.

'Not today,' she said, 'I really am in a hurry. But I'll come back. I'll definitely come back to look at it, now that I know it's here.'

'The other employee who works here might be reluctant to show it to you. She can be difficult.'

'Thank you very much,' Claire said. 'I'll be back.'

After she was gone, whistling a sentimental tune, the young man decided that it was unusual for such an attractive woman to be so low-key.

* * *

Claire walked home slowly, thinking that she had done the right thing not to pry more deeply into her mother's life. There would have been something unsavory about it while her mother lay in bed, ill. Maybe later, but not now. The possibility that she and Gabrielle might be Roberto Goldini's daughters – and not Selim Sahli's – crossed her mind; it left her more curious than upset. Should she be telling Gabrielle about her discovery? Probably not, she concluded. Gabrielle would take it hard.

What Claire could not fathom was why her mother had not made up some story about her past – any story – as opposed to keeping mum about it, as she had all those years. She found this blanket of silence inexplicable.

Surely her father would have known that there was something murky about her mother's past for why else had he accepted – perhaps even encouraged – her being so silent about it? Had he actually known about Roberto Goldoni's existence?

Probably out of respect for their older brother, family solidarity and to protect her and Gabrielle, whatever her uncles and aunt knew, they had kept to themselves. And yet, in a memorable scene, when she was considering leaving Alexandre, her Uncle Yussef had seemed on the verge of revealing something to her, saying that, if she was so willing to flout social conventions, maybe he should be telling her a story he was not sure she would want to hear. Shaken, she had nevertheless replied that she would not be bullied. On her way out of his office, she had wondered whether he had been about to tell her that her parents were not married. It all came back to her now: the scene, her uncle's threat and her speculation. She had entertained that possibility, but rejected it in favor of the hypothesis that they had married after Gabrielle's birth. That Gabrielle's baptism was a few days after her fourth birthday – unusually late – seemed to her, at the time, to support the hypothesis.

Still walking slowly, Claire recalled the few summers her mother had agreed to accompany her father on his trips to Europe, taking her and Gabrielle along. Her mother was never satisfied with the hotels, no matter how good. She seemed content when they first set foot in their rooms, but the next day or the day after, she would begin finding fault with the hotel: the restaurant was too noisy, the rooms too drafty or too hot, the cleaning staff not conscientious enough. It would not take long before she suggested trying another hotel. So the trips meant to give them pleasure – her father loved traveling and his enthusiasm was contagious – would end up being stressful for the four of them.

One summer, they were in Venice at the Hotel Danieli. The day after their arrival, her mother had observed over dinner that the staff were not so friendly, causing her father to lose his legendary calm and nearly shout, 'But Letitia, of what importance is this? We're in Italy! In Venice! Isn't this what counts?' Her mother had said, apologetically, 'I'm sorry Selim, but you know me, I'm only comfortable between my own walls. I'm nervous when I travel. I cannot seem to help it.' And he had said, his tone back to normal, 'When I'm in Italy, I feel especially close to you.' Claire still vividly remembered that exchange and feeling equally sorry for both.

It was during that summer that her mother had bought herself, in Paris, a dress for Yussef Sahli's wedding. The wedding promised to be the social event of the season in Cairo. Her father had been eager for all four of them to search for something in the city's leading fashion houses. The one dress that immediately took Letitia's fancy – empire-style yet with a modest décolleté – was two-layered and made of blue gauze and beige lace. To wear it well a woman had to be as delicate as her. 'With this dress, hardly any jewelry is needed,' Letitia had remarked when trying it on, in front of her admiring family.

'Surely, a little something though,' Selim had suggested.

'It has to be little or else it will detract from the dress,' she had said, causing them both to laugh. Then, she, normally quite restrained, had pirouetted across the room.

At the wedding, eleven-year-old Gabrielle would stand proudly by her mother's side, basking in the compliments attracted by the dress. All excited, she had asked her mother, 'At your wedding, Mother, what sort of dresses did women wear?' Instead of answering, Letitia had drawn Gabrielle's and Claire's attention to the bride's sister. 'What do you think of her dress?' she had asked them. 'I like yours better,' Gabrielle had said, in the best of dispositions towards her mother. This scene too, Claire remembered well. To wear with the dress, her father had given her mother a diamond pendant bearing the inscription, 'More than yesterday, less than tomorrow.'

Passing again by the newspaper vendor, Claire nodded for the second time to his wife now suckling her baby. 'But Yasmine,' she heard the husband protest, 'that baby has had more than enough! Does he really need to be fed every half hour?' So the woman's name was Yasmine. Claire felt something akin to embarrassment that this woman, with whom she had exchanged greetings over the course of much of their lives, had been for her a face without a name.

Further down the *midan*, around the barracks, there was no sign of demonstrations.

As she approached the marble fountain at the entrance of her building, Claire was greeted effusively by one of the doormen. Because her Uncle Yussef owned the building, the doormen tended to be overzealous in her presence.

The doorman opened the elevator for Claire. A young man followed her.

'Where to, God willing?' the doorman growled at the young man.

Claire picked up some hesitation in the man's voice when he answered, 'The eighth floor.'

'To see whom?' the doorman shouted.

'My cousin Magdi,' the young man said, this time with more self-assurance.

The doorman closed the elevator door, mumbling, 'Which Magdi? There are several Magdis in the building.'

Claire lived on the fourth floor. The elevator was slow. By the time it reached the first floor, the young man had unbuttoned his fly and exposed himself.

Not a word, he said.

Not a word, she said.

Turning sideways, she pretended to look at herself in the mirror. Revulsion – not fear – was what she felt. She could have yelled for the doorman who would have heard her. She did not yell. All she did was keep her eyes fixed on the mirror.

When the elevator stopped on the fourth floor, the young man opened the elevator door and held it for Claire. She presumed that he had re-buttoned his fly. 'Thank you,' she said.

The absurdity of her 'Thank you' struck her only once she was out of the elevator.

Her mother was dozing by the time she was back home.

'She has been humming in her sleep,' Om Batta told Claire.

* * *

Om Batta gone, Claire got a shoebox down from the top of a large armoire in her bedroom. Upon moving in with her, her mother had entrusted her with it saying, 'I give it to you and not to Gabrielle because she believes in getting rid of things, anything that causes clutter. You like to hang on to things.'

Later that day, before going to bed, Claire took a small stack of letters out of the shoebox. The letters, from her father to her mother, were written while he was in Europe for treatment. She had glanced at them a while back, though without particular interest. Now she meant to look for some mention of, or allusion to, her mother's life with Roberto Goldoni. She did have some qualms about reading their correspondence – the same sort that had kept her from looking at the file at the consulate. But this time her curiosity prevailed.

She read each letter – seventeen in all. Nothing in them pointed to the existence of a Roberto Goldoni.

In the letters, her father addressed her mother as 'Darling Letitia', or as 'My sweet little wife', 'My darling wife', or 'My very cherished wife'. He referred to her and Gabrielle as 'our darling daughters', 'our precious ones', or 'our devilish little ones!' He often ended his letters by signing 'Your loving husband.'

Might he have been using these terms in a broad sense, wanting to reassure his partner that, to him, they were husband and wife, no matter what? Was this how she was to interpret, for example, a letter sent from Vittel in August 1913, in which he was chiding Letitia for having concealed from him that Gabrielle was sick? He wrote in that letter:

My darling Letitia,

You are not a child; I am not one either. You and I have reached an age where subterfuges are quite unnecessary. Furthermore, husband and wife should hide nothing from each other, particularly where their children are concerned. An hour before the boat left, when it would have been very easy for me to disembark, I received a telegram from you assuring me that Gabrielle was doing well. That telegram accomplished its purpose: when the ship sailed, my mind was at rest. Then Zaki arrived in Vittel. He informed me that Gabrielle was still running a high fever when he left and the doctor had been seeing her every day. You imagine my state! I then received a letter from Naum confirming what Zaki said. So I sent you the two telegrams to which you responded by trying to reassure me, but are you giving me the whole picture? I come back to what I said at the beginning of this letter. We are neither children nor strangers to each other. You should have let me know, the morning of my departure, that our child was still sick. I would have returned home. I would have wanted to! Now tell me the truth, has Gabrielle fully recovered? If there is any doubt, send me a telegram.

I fear you don't fully appreciate how much each one of you means to me though you ought to. You ought to know you occupy a pre-eminent place in your husband's heart. How could you not after our twelve years of living side by side, tasting the bitterness and sweetness of life ...

Please, do tell me the truth – by telegram if need be. I beg you to.

Zaki said the doctor recommends you go to Alexandria for a few days with the children. I see no reason for you not to go, although, knowing you, you might find the choice of a hotel daunting. If you decide to go, I can tell Yussef to book hotel rooms, if that's what you would like.

I hate being so cut off from you and the children. I feel lonely no matter how many people I meet and how pleasant their company is.

Your loving but worried
Selim

Claire read that letter several times, looking for some hidden meaning. None jumped at her.

At the bottom of the shoebox she found a passport of her mother's, which she had missed last time she looked. The passport, issued in Constantinople in October 1901, was valid for three years and was provided for the purpose of allowing Letitia – who was twenty-two at the time – to travel to Piraeus. Stamped in the passport was a visa for Cairo, issued in May 1902.

Claire had no idea that her mother had spent time in Constantinople. Written in 1913, her father's letter from Vittel had him and her mother already living together in 1901 since he referred to their having lived together for twelve years. Yet, according to Letitia's passport, she was in Constantinople in 1901. Was it there then – and not in Venice – that she met Selim? It could not have been in Egypt, her visa for Cairo having been issued in 1902. Did Selim make a mistake about the number of years they had been living together? He was a very precise man though.

Claire gave up trying to put the pieces of the puzzle together. The sequence of events did suggest, however, that she and Gabrielle were Selim Sahli's daughters since Selim and Letitia had apparently been living together long before Gabrielle was born.

Claire's other finds in the shoebox were two photos: one of her mother's father signed 'To my darling daughter, Letitia.' The photo showed a man with a graying beard but a youthful and lively expression, wearing a military uniform and a cap on which a red cross was sewn, from which Claire deduced that he might have been a medical officer. The other photo was of an adolescent boy, around fifteen or sixteen, in a stylish suit. Fair and blue-eyed, the boy looked quite formal; he was wearing a cravat and the corner of a white handkerchief showed from the pocket of his suit jacket. Her mother's brother? Roberto Goldoni?

She was studying that picture when Alexandre, just back from another late meeting with her Uncle Yussef barged into her room, looking worried. 'Darling,' he said, 'your mother seems to be having difficulties breathing. I was going to the kitchen to get myself a drink of water when I heard her breathing hard. You ought to call the doctor first thing in the morning.'

Letitia's breathing was irregular; she seemed to be gasping for breath. Claire pulled an armchair close to the couch and sat up with her all night long.

Early on in the night, Letitia asked Claire whether Osta Osman had sent them dried dates from Nubia, as had become his custom in the early fall. Then, much later, she murmured twice, 'What a complicated life.'

As the night progressed, Claire would relive the moments she and Gabrielle had spent with their father the day he died. And though she loved her mother, she was beset with the same thought that had so troubled her in the wake of her father's death: if a choice had to be made, he was the one who should have lived. Twenty-two years later, Claire reached that same conclusion, with more sadness, yet, in a way, more detachment, than she had as a young girl.

Dawn came; her mother's breathing was still labored and she was sweating.

'Mother,' Claire said softly, 'what would you think of spending a few days in the hospital? They would check you out thoroughly.'

Her mother shook her head. 'No, no,' she said, 'I won't go to the hospital. Please, Claire, keep me here.' Then, she said, 'When the time comes – very soon I hope – I want no obituary notice.'

* * *

Letitia went downhill fast.

The two doctors were called again. They seemed perplexed. 'It could be pneumonia,' each said in a tone that failed to inspire Claire with confidence.

A bone specialist sent by Bella's husband came. He looked preoccupied after examining Letitia. Out in the hallway, he said to Claire and Gabrielle, 'You should have called me earlier, although I'm not sure that it would have made much difference.'

'But what happened, doctor? She wasn't well, but she wasn't so bad either,' Gabrielle asked. The specialist gave her a look that put her on the defensive. 'She really wasn't so bad,' Gabrielle repeated.

Gazing at her, the specialist stated, 'I'm not a believer in putting on kid gloves to talk to the families of my patients. It's a cancer that has metastasized.'

Flustered, Gabrielle said, 'We had no idea, doctor! No idea! The doctors who have been seeing her never mentioned that possibility.'

Shaking his head, the specialist said, 'Mistakes are made. A diagnosis is never a sure thing. I may be wrong. The next few days will be telling. At this stage, the important thing is to minimize her discomfort. I suggest strong sedatives.'

'Even though she's so frail?' Gabrielle exclaimed, her question more a protest than a query.

'I don't want her to suffer. I am all for strong sedatives,' Claire said, ignoring her sister's objections.

'Strong sedatives might kill her,' Gabrielle bellowed and stormed out of the hallway.

Shifting from cold and impersonal to warm, the specialist adopted a fatherly tone. 'It will take a little while for your sister to digest what's happening. Her reaction is not uncommon.'

After he was gone, Claire found Gabrielle on the balcony.

'I should have been more vigilant. I blame myself for not having done more,' Claire told her sister.

'I'll spend the night here. We can take turns sitting up with her,' Gabrielle stated in an unusually subdued voice. She suggested, 'Tomorrow we should try to find a nurse. I'll call the French and

Italian hospitals. They might know of someone willing to do night shifts.'

'Good idea,' Claire said.

'Do you want Nicolas to fetch Simone from Constance's place? She could spend a few nights at our place. Aida has been clamoring for her.'

'It would upset Constance,' Claire said. 'You know how much she loves to have Simone and Aida spend time at her place.'

Gabrielle shrugged. 'You're far too accommodating of Constance,' she said.

'Constance does not have an easy life. If she gets some pleasure out of looking after Simone, I see no reason to deny her that pleasure.'

'Except that it gives her reasons to meddle in affairs that are not hers.'

'It's not so bad, really,' Claire stated.

'As you please, then!' Gabrielle said curtly.

Within a few hours of the specialist's visit, Letitia stopped talking altogether. She seemed lucid, responded to questions, nodding and shaking her head for 'yes' and 'no,' but she would not speak. She was awake much of the time. Claire gave her some sedatives, though less than the dose prescribed. When she asked whether she was in much discomfort, Letitia gestured with her hand, 'so-so.'

Shortly before noon, Iris came for a visit with a box full of her aunt's favorite almond cookies. When shown the cookies, Letitia put on the ghost of a smile and reached for Iris's hand.

Told by Alexandre that his sister-in-law was sliding fast, Yussef Sahli called every hour, taking the opportunity just about every time to question the specialist's competence. 'A charlatan probably,' he kept saying over the phone. That the specialist had come recommended by his son-in-law Aristote, was a big strike against the man as far as Yussef was concerned. Yussef Sahli had never quite swallowed his daughter Bella's marriage to Aristote who did not care a wit about money and tended to be more amused than intimidated by his father-in-law.

It was just about to get dark – that time of the evening when, if alone, Claire often felt unsettled and had vague longings. While keeping watch over her mother, she realized, for the first time in her life, the strangeness of having grown up, in a society in which connections and background meant everything, next to a loving and tender mother, whose identity was such a complete black hole; about whose past she knew virtually nothing. Considered by Gabrielle and the Sahlis as weak and fragile, her mother must have had a certain strength of character to have kept as silent as she had all those years.

If her mother had been in better health, would Claire have mentioned her discovery at the consulate, she wondered? Should she be asking her now, 'Mother, is there anything you wish to tell me?' Might Letitia surprise her and answer? It seemed to Claire that asking her any such question now would be both cruel and futile. Her mother's past no longer really mattered; little would change in her and Gabrielle's life from knowledge of that past, however much such knowledge might explain her mother's timidity, bouts of melancholy, and occasional odd behavior.

* * *

Letitia died at daybreak, three days after the specialist's visit, while her daughters were having coffee in the kitchen.

Her funeral was held at the Roman Catholic Church of St. Joseph, in the heart of Cairo. All the Sahlis – with the exception of the one living in Paris – attended the funeral. So did Ali and Om Batta with her son Mahmud. Batta stayed at Claire's place to look after Simone and Aida.

Just before the ceremony, the priest, who barely knew Letitia – she was not much of a churchgoer – asked Claire and Gabrielle to tell him what sort of woman she was; he needed to know for the homily. 'Devoted to her family,' Gabrielle said laconically. Claire added, 'She was very affected by our father's death; she never really recovered from it.' Claire saw Gabrielle wince as she said this.

The only ones to cry during the ceremony were Iris, Constance and Om Batta.

After Letitia's burial in the Sahli crypt, Iris embraced Claire and whispered, 'I am so sorry, I know how attached you were to her. She was like a reed, a fragile reed.'

Claire whispered back, 'In truth, Iris, I feel more grief thinking of her life than of her death.'

When it was her turn to pay her respects, Om Batta took Claire to one side and said in a low voice, 'I know that it's very hard for a daughter to lose a mother, but it was time for her to go. I did not want to tell you the day I came for a visit, but I had a dream about her in which she was reunited with Selim Bey. That's why I hurried to see her. I have known her for much of my life. She was like an older sister to me.' Om Batta paused to wipe some tears, then went on, 'It was time really. She was getting confused. When I sat with her, I tried to cheer her up by talking about Simone and Aida so I told her that Selim Bey would have been extremely proud of his granddaughters, and she said to me, "Yes, Roberto would have been proud."'

Claire asked softly, 'She said "Roberto"?'

'She was tired by then. I had tired her out. You know how I tend to go on and on. She is in peace now. I envy her. I hope it's my turn next.'

'Don't say so!' Claire said. 'You're far too young for that.'

'I don't feel it,' Om Batta sighed and hugged Claire. She walked out of the cemetery, leaning against her son.

After hugging his two nieces, Yussef Sahli said in a loud voice, 'This specialist was really a bird of bad omen!'

Neither at the funeral, nor after it, did anybody raise the question of an obituary notice – not even Gabrielle.

* * *

Not quite three months after Letitia's death, on an unseasonably cold early December morning, Claire and Iris arranged over the phone to meet at eleven o'clock in the morning at Groppi's.

Preying on Iris's mind was Anastase's growing conviction that they ought to leave Egypt. He had been saying for some time that there was no room for people like them in the country. Whenever he heard him express that view, Yussef Sahli would boil inside but try not to explode; he was on tense enough terms with his other son-in-law to antagonize Anastase, whom he considered saintly for putting up with Iris's disabling asthma and unconventional character.

Yet, at a recent family lunch attended by Claire, upon overhearing Anastase tell the person sitting next to him that the Syro-Lebanese in Egypt belonged only marginally more in the country than the

Greeks and the Italians, Yussef Sahli had not managed to contain himself. Interrupting his son-in-law, he had asserted loudly that it was entirely Anastase's problem if he felt that he did not belong in Egypt. Greeks were notorious for being insular, he said. In reality, Anastase did not feel Greek any more than he felt Egyptian. Unlike his brother-in-law Aristote, who was solidly anchored in Egypt's Greek community, he wore his Greekness lightly and mixed in wide circles, perhaps in part because of the nature of the business he owned, a company that imported tobacco and manufactured cigarettes, for sale in Egypt and abroad.

Anastase, an unflappable sort, had taken his father-in-law's loud and aggressive expression of displeasure with a smile. Iris, however, never missed a chance to disagree with her father. So she argued with him, although she was not that fond of Anastase's views.

'Fundamentally, he does not like me, and I don't like him either,' she often told Claire, something she reiterated on the phone that morning. 'He's the kind of man I would have nothing to do with, if he were not my father. If for no other reason than to put a certain distance between the two of us, leaving Egypt might be a good thing, although I would hate to be far from you and from Mother.'

At a quarter to eleven, on her way to Groppi's, Claire stopped to buy a paper from the newspaper vendor at the corner of the *midan* and Suleiman Pasha Street. An icy wind was blowing. She turned up the velvet collar of her new black coat – a present from her Uncle Yussef.

'Where is your wife today?' she asked the newspaper vendor, who was by himself.

'At home', he said, 'the baby has a bad cold. She thought that it would be better to keep him home.'

'She's right, I hope he gets better quickly,' Claire said with real concern. Whenever she crossed the *midan*, she had grown accustomed to seeing the big and placid baby in his mother's arms, on her lap, or at her breast.

With its majestic pillars encased in marble, its terrazzo floors and its twenty-foot-high ceilings, Groppi Suleiman Pasha had been the subject of rapt descriptions for its opulent art deco style at the time of its inauguration in 1925. Still grand twenty-one years later, its main attraction for Claire and Iris was its vicinity to Claire's apartment and the downtown bookstores.

Iris was already at Groppi's and seated by the time Claire arrived. Both from her expression and from the fact that she was on time, which was unprecedented, Claire guessed that something was amiss.

The two cousins kissed.

Without further ado, Iris announced, 'I can barely stay! My father called me half an hour ago to say that he would be having lunch with Swiss friends of his who are in town, and I must join them because he might have to leave half-way through the lunch. The nerve that man has! He didn't even ask me if I'm free – let alone interested. This man thinks he owns people. The only one he does not dare deal with in that fashion is Mother.' Iris paused before saying, in a sour tone that surprised Claire, 'Mind you, he is careful with Bella too.' She took a cigarette box out of her handbag, offered a cigarette to Claire, who declined, lit one for herself only to blow it out, explaining, with a giggle, 'I'm trying to stop but I'm also trying to lose some weight.' Relaxing somewhat, she went on, 'You look wonderful, Claire. Really wonderful. You had me quite concerned three months ago. I had never seen you look tired before.' Then she let out, 'I miss Aunt Letitia, I do.'

'You were her favorite niece,' Claire said.

'It's good to hear that. I liked her a lot.' Her voice now husky, Iris continued, 'Well, will you be ordering hot chocolate or let yourself be tempted by an ice cream? How about Aunt Letitia's favorite, *sfogliatella*?' With a small laugh, again nervous-sounding, she admitted to having already ordered for herself a chocolate ice cream with a double portion of crème chantilly. 'You know me; my dieting resolutions are never long-lived,' she said self-deprecatingly.

A tall woman, in her late twenties, with a healthy, somewhat ruddy complexion and ash-blond hair, Iris was on the heavy side. Perhaps because of her brusque gestures and heavy-footed gait, people tended to find her masculine, yet her face was soft, feminine. Extremely nearsighted, she wore thick glasses about which she was self-conscious. The glasses did detract from her looks as they concealed her best feature: expressive hazel eyes.

'I'll have a chocolate ice cream too,' Claire said with unusual decisiveness as she summoned a waiter. 'I was dying for a chocolate ice cream on my way here.'

After Iris left, Claire looked through the paper. The news was mostly about the new government, the collapse of talks over British withdrawal, and the Sudan question. Egypt's strong man, Sidqi, had failed. There had been a fresh outbreak of student demonstrations, in which streetcars had been overturned and set on fire, and English books burned. A couple of articles on Palestine caught Claire's attention. She read them attentively.

'I could easily eat another ice cream,' Claire thought, blushing slightly. She seemed to be having a craving not unlike those she had when pregnant with Simone. Could it be?

She did not know why but suddenly she wanted to read her mother's file at the Italian consulate She looked at her watch. There was still time before the consulate closed for lunch.

* * *

Letitia Graziano had a younger sister called Chiara and a younger brother called Massimo. When Letitia was six years old, her father, by then already a widower, took up residence in Massawa, in Eritrea, with his three children. In 1896, at the age of eighteen, Letitia married Roberto Goldoni, a resident of Massawa. He was originally from Volterra. Two years later, the couple separated and Letitia left Eritrea. In 1902 the couple reunited in Cairo. Their reconciliation was short-lived. Within a year, Letitia left her husband and vanished. That was what Roberto Goldoni stated at the Italian consulate in Cairo in 1912, when he went to report that his wife was missing. The consulate then embarked on a search. It first contacted her two siblings in Eritrea. They wrote back to say that they had no idea of her whereabouts, that she had never written to them since leaving Eritrea; after their father's death in 1908, his estate had been divided between the two of them as no one knew if she was still alive. The consulate's next step was to contact other Italian consulates – in France and Greece – to check whether they had any information about missing Letitia. The consulates reported nothing whatsoever on Letitia Graziano. In June 1940, the Italian consular tribunal in Cairo declared Letitia Graziano presumed dead. The declaration was officially recorded five years later in the journal of the mixed tribunals and took retroactive effect. Roberto Goldoni remarried in 1947. He died that same year, in Cairo's Italian hospital.

So Letitia had grown up in Eritrea, had married at eighteen, had left her husband, and made a new life for herself with another man – a new life within reach of that husband who claimed he had no idea where she was gone, and within walking distance of the consulate that declared her dead in 1940.

As it turns out, Claire would learn none of this that cold December day in 1946. When she arrived at the consulate, it was packed. The cooperative young employee was away from his desk. The woman to whom she talked insisted that, without prior authorization from the consul, she could not show her the file.

* * *

Years would pass before Claire finally read the file. When she did, it would be by chance.

She was at the consulate in 1961 to inquire about getting an Italian passport when the employee she had dealt with in 1946, still working at the consulate and still a touch taken with her, mentioned the day she had sought out her mother's file. That he should have remembered took her aback. As impulsively as she had that one time, she asked him if she could look at the file again – a request he joked about, saying, 'By now, it's become archival material, but I'll see what I can do.'

What would fifty-one-year-old Claire feel upon finally reading the file? To describe it as 'archival material' was actually quite appropriate, her present world bore so little resemblance to her past. She felt surprisingly disconnected from it.

She would be left, however, with a sense of intellectual frustration as she was still unable to put the pieces of the puzzle together. Had Roberto Goldoni known, all along, where Letitia resided yet told the consulate that she had vanished simply to have his marriage dissolved and be free to remarry? Had her father and Goldoni known each other, or about each other? Had her father bought Goldoni's silence and perhaps even plotted with him to gain Letitia's freedom? Was her father's duel related to her mother's past? The main actors in the drama were dead. So were those – her uncles and her aunt – who might have had a peripheral role in it, except for her Uncle Yussef who was recovering from a slight cerebral attack so in no state to be quizzed about the subject.

For Claire, instead of providing answers, the file compounded the questions, although it did shed light on a small matter. As she was handing the file back, Claire suddenly remembered her mother's riding outfit, the outfit that she and Gabrielle had discovered at the bottom of a trunk when they were little girls. This outfit made more sense now. The setting in which her mother had grown up – colonial Eritrea – was a natural setting for horse riding.

The memory of that riding outfit would cause Claire to feel a surge of renewed compassion for her mother and sadness at how her life had unfolded. In the grip of that sadness, she would remember her mother's penultimate utterance, 'What a complicated life.' And she would wonder, in hindsight, whether that statement might have been an invitation for questions to be asked – an invitation she had failed to recognize.

1947: Yves

The year 1947 saw no reduction in Egypt's political agitation. Bombs exploded in Cairo and Alexandria. Committees of all sorts – of Muslim youth, of young Egyptians, of liberation, of women's groups, of united workers – popped up. In a manifesto published by the press, the Muslim Brotherhood told the Egyptian people that, if they wanted the British to leave and real independence, they had no option but to fight, cautioning them though against rash action and snap uprisings. The message was thus ambiguous.

In certain circles, rumors began circulating that the government was about to order the dissolution of the Muslim Brotherhood and ban its activities. On May 6, 1947, the anniversary of King Faruq's accession to the throne, a bomb exploded in the Metro cinema in downtown Cairo, killing a spectator and injuring several others. A historian lamented that, rather than being its manifestation, the violence attested to the failure of the nationalist movement. He and others recalled with a nostalgia that was bound to color their judgement – as nostalgia always does – the spirit that had suffused the nationalist fervor of 1919, deeming it to have been infinitely more constructive than the prevailing mood. These were the days when the ideal of parliamentary democracy meant something, they now believed.

For Claire, the year began on a radiant note. She was pregnant. Her desire to have as many children as possible – an almost all-consuming desire after Guy's death – had been granted a second time at not such a young age. She was thirty-seven years old.

She had already picked a name: 'Yves' – a name she thought would suit a vivacious and quick little boy, as she hoped hers would be. Alexandre would likely want to name him Constantin, after his father. So, on paper, the baby – if a boy– would be either 'Constantin Yves' or 'Yves Constantin,' but she was sure that the family, Alexandre included, would call him 'Yves.'

The political situation concerned Claire. It both concerned her and confused her. She remembered the twenties as a time when just about everyone around her was touched by nationalist fervor. Now, in her circles, many of her friends and acquaintances were saying that the new generation of nationalists was becoming rudderless and uncontrollable. Was the current political agitation perceived in those circles as posing a fundamental threat to their existence? If so, it was not an issue that was put right on the table, not even by Anastase whose contention was not so much that privilege was about to come under attack, nor that Egypt's partly Egyptianized minorities were suddenly vulnerable, but that these minorities were in a false situation in the country and had always been so. His was an existential malaise shared by Claire and heightened, in her case, by the feeling that the life that she had managed to stitch for herself was based on a precarious equilibrium and lacked legitimacy on several fronts. Besides feeling like an interloper in her country, she felt like one in her social set. With some of the trappings of privilege, her life lacked its basis, namely wealth, of which neither she nor Alexandre possessed the slightest amount. That this was no secret in the moneyed society she frequented and did not seem to be held against her did ease her sense of not quite belonging to it. Her singular grace, engaging manners and good looks always guaranteed her a warm reception in that set. Alexandre's gradual withdrawal from it for lack of enough means made it, however, more and more difficult for her to hold on to her social life. Yet she did, finessing her marital situation with the dexterity of a tight-rope walker only to be gripped every now and then by the feeling that her life had a pretend quality that threatened to become its defining character. Knowledge of the mysterious nature of her parents' union – even if it had not shaken her to the core – could not but contribute to that feeling.

For all these reasons, Claire sometimes found herself actually cheering for the men and women in the street. On some level, she identified with them, even though she realized that, should things go wrong for the world in which she lived – albeit on such an uncertain footing – she stood to lose more than her cousins and friends. They had assets and husbands young enough to move to some other country and start afresh, whereas she would likely be locked in Egypt.

In her imagination, her son – she had nearly convinced herself it would be a boy – would make himself a life in France. She was determined to do everything in her power to that end. She hoped that Simone too would settle abroad, but, for the boy yet to be born, her wish was yet firmer: he must escape her world – a world in which she did not feel true to herself.

* * *

Half-way through August of that year, in time for the birth of Claire's baby, Iris returned to Cairo from Switzerland, where she had spent a month for her asthma. In addition to the several baby outfits she had knitted, Iris gave Claire a leather-bound diary to keep a record of the small and big events in the baby's first year, something Claire had not done after Simone's birth and wished she had.

There was a chance the baby's birth would coincide with the anniversary of Letitia's death. Claire was hoping not. Her wish was granted: Yves Constantin Conti was born on September first, ten days before the first anniversary of the death of his maternal grandmother. It was an easy and quick birth. Long-legged, wiry and very alert, the boy was a good weight: 7 pounds 10 ounces. He was born with a crop of bushy, black hair that had the same texture as that of his Aunt Gabrielle, who immediately called attention to the similarity.

'So it's a boy! Well done!' Claire's Uncle Yussef wrote on the congratulatory card he sent to the hospital with a huge bouquet of flowers – one of many bouquets, including twenty-four roses from Alexandre's first cousin George Conti, a wealthy man, married but with neither children nor nephews. Did it occur to Claire or Alexandre that, under Egyptian law, a son of theirs would stand to inherit from George Conti? If it did, they never discussed the subject. They knew that, for many years, George Conti had wanted offspring – above all, a son – and had only recently resigned himself to the prospect of remaining childless. So when his roses were delivered to Claire's room, she remarked to Alexandre and Constance who was quite fond of her cousin George, 'It must be hard for him.'

* * *

September 4

The delivery was so incredibly easy and the baby in such good health that they sent me back home earlier than planned. Little Yves is a delightful baby. He is not a big eater though. But neither was Simone. Curiously, he seemed to have more appetite right after the birth. When I mentioned this to the nurses, they joked about my being overprotective. He is awake for much of the day and watches attentively all that is going on around him. When he sleeps, he sleeps soundly. Better than Simone used to. She is very interested in him and has yet to manifest any jealousy. She is keen on showing him her picture books and giving him some of her toys. Did Dr. Spock exaggerate the extent of sibling rivalry?

It's too soon to say whom he looks like. His hair feels like Gabrielle's. I hope it stays that way.

Alexandre is being ultra-attentive and Constance is in seventh heaven. It's obvious that she would have loved to have children. That she takes such pleasure in her brothers' children, showing no envy whatsoever, speaks incredibly well of her. She would have been a good mother – certainly nurturing. Iris too loves children and would love to have a child, although it seems doubtful she ever will. She is on so much medication. I worry about her. Thank God for Anastase. He is good to her and for her.

I'm happy. Very, very happy.

September 5

I'm feeling tired. Little Yves does not eat much so I have decided to breastfeed him whenever he is hungry. He has extraordinarily long lashes – long and curly. And bushy eyebrows as black as his hair, which he has yet to lose. He has a delicious dimple on his chin. His ears though are quite a sight: they're huge and stick out. Simone's were so tiny. When I look at him, he gazes back, as if he is studying my every feature. He rarely cries, but when he does, he is extremely loud. The nurses in the hospital remarked on that. They told me, 'Your son will be a man of extremes, quiet and self-contained, yet with an explosive side. You'll see.'

'Your son' – how I like the sound of those two words!

Iris spent the whole afternoon here – mostly admiring the baby, though she did make a point of doing a puzzle with Simone, who is remarkably good with puzzles. Iris was very impressed.

September 6

I have been having difficulties feeding Yves so I called the hospital to ask for advice. I talked to the head nurse. She offered to send me a nurse to watch me feed him. She thinks I'm out of practice. She has a brusque manner of speaking that is off-putting. I reminded her that it has not been that long since I breastfed Simone. She must have realized she had been offhand because her tone then changed and she tried to reassure me about Yves, saying he is a very healthy baby.

September 7

The nurse came early this morning. Her name is Alba – an uncommon but beautiful name. She is pretty and outgoing. I told her that the baby had lost a few ounces. She said that this was not unusual. She watched me breastfeed and could see for herself that the baby was not overly interested. She suggested we try the bottle. He did drink a bit though not much and regurgitated a lot. We agreed that we should try a combination of breastfeeding and the bottle. Earlier in the day, Gabrielle had suggested I switch entirely to the bottle. She may be right. I'll see how it goes over the next few days.

I'm still tired. Simone has been out of sorts for much of the day. No doubt, she has picked up on my concern about the baby's feeding. Constance took her out for an ice cream in the evening and that seemed to settle her down.

Alexandre came back home today with two absolutely magnificent dolls – one for Simone and one for Aida. As usual, he goes all out when he buys presents. He never buys something for Simone without buying the same thing for Aida. I'm sure that Nicolas and Gabrielle will disapprove, as they did when he bought each of the two girls a train set for no special occasion. I can hear Gabrielle objecting that he can do as he pleases with Simone, but she does not want him to spoil Aida.

September 8
The baby is eating less and less – no matter how I feed him. He's also sleeping more than usual and when he cries, he doesn't cry as loudly. I'm beginning to panic. Simone's paediatrician is out of town. So is Aristote. There's a small chance that he'll be back tomorrow. Iris thinks he might. Alexandre has offered to call Dr. Thilos, an acquaintance of his. I have no idea how good a doctor he is. All I know is that he's a good bridge player. I suppose it won't hurt to have him drop by.

Dr. Thilos came while we were having dinner half an hour ago. He was on his way to the Greek Club and in a hurry. He arrived at 8:30 P.M. and left twenty minutes later. He spoke of a possible milk intolerance and said that he would drop by early in the week. He left it vague when exactly that might be. I was not impressed. He is casual and condescending. When the time came to pay him for the consultation, he charged us a regular doctor's fee yet managed somehow to make us feel that he was doing us a big favor. Well, I suppose it is Sunday!

After he was gone, I spent a good hour trying to feed Yves. Later, Simone woke up, all upset. She had had a nightmare. She went back to sleep only after I read to her her favorite Babar story. I also promised her to have Aida come over tomorrow.

I woke up several times at night to check on little Yves. I tried to feed him a bit without much success. He's sleeping now. It's four o'clock in the morning. I'll take a quick peek at him, then try to rest for a couple of hours.

How quickly one becomes attached to a human being. It's frightening.

September 9

Another nurse from the hospital came by this morning. I had not expected her but was pleased to see her. She seemed surprised to hear that I was still having difficulties feeding the baby. 'He does not look unwell,' she said. I did not like her tone. She sounded flippant. I told her that he was definitely less alert than he had been. She suggested we try to feed him. I gave her the bottle. She had as little success as I. She ventured the opinion that he probably prefers to be breastfed. I told her that, breast or bottle, it made no difference. To avoid getting into an argument with her, I cut the conversation short. By that stage, I wanted her to leave.

Iris is supposed to come for lunch. I think I'll cancel. I'm too preoccupied.

It is ten o'clock at night. It feels like I spent the whole day trying to feed the baby. I cannot do it anymore. I want him examined at the hospital.

September 10
In the middle of the night, I noticed that the baby's stools had changed color. The baby is now in the hospital, I'm so upset, so upset.

September 11
What is it that they missed seeing in the hospital, after he was born, that this odious Dr. Thilos overlooked when I sensed, almost right from the outset, that something was not quite right? I should have taken the baby to the hospital as soon as I noticed that he wasn't feeding properly. I should have!

Yesterday was a terrible day and today is no better. It started with my calling that horrible Dr. Thilos, at seven o'clock in the morning. After I had described to him the baby's stools, he barked over the phone, 'Why didn't you call me earlier?' I almost hung up on him and told Alexandre, who was standing in the hallway, to take the baby to the Italian hospital right away. It was not until I had bundled up the baby in a blanket that I decided to stay at home with Simone.

I have been calling the hospital every hour or so. The baby is still in intensive care. The head nurse said they're doing all they can. The doctor in charge can be reached in a couple of hours. I keep on changing my mind about going to the hospital. One minute I am all set to go, then I am frightened. I cannot bear the thought of losing him and of being there when it happens.

Even Iris, my unconditional supporter, seems disconcerted by my reaction – my not being by his side. Chain-smoking and looking at me with enormous concern, she spent the evening here yesterday. I would have preferred to be alone.

Constance is at the hospital right now. Gabrielle will be going this afternoon.

Today is the anniversary of Mother's death.

September 13

It's all over. I never got to see him. I never went to the hospital.

The thought that I did not deserve him does not leave me.

September 14

Gabrielle and Alexandre are sorting out the funeral arrange-ments. He was baptized in the hospital. With Alexandre's approval, Gabrielle had arranged for a priest to come. He'll be buried in the Conti crypt. I'm letting them make all the deci-sions, none of which seems of any consequence to me. They're putting an obituary notice in the papers.

Everyone is silent about my desertion of the baby, deeming it, I am sure, too terrible a subject to raise. Too much of a heart or too little? I don't know. I don't understand myself. I have nothing to say in my defense.

Om Batta came in the morning and said the usual words of condolence, 'It was God's will.' She went on to say that children are not always a source of joy, that one never knows how things will turn out with them, that some can even end up destroying their parents. I think that she was referring to

her own situation, but I did not feel up to asking her. Gabrielle
was present when Om Batta said these things. I could tell, from
Gabrielle's expression, that she was about to usher her out of the
room so I asked Om Batta to have a cup of coffee with me. Om
Batta's presence was soothing to me. Perhaps because she's also
unhappy.

September 16
The baby was buried in the Conti crypt. On the way to the
church, I said unforgivable words to Alexandre. I sobbed out,
'But for me, nobody wanted this baby.' He looked crestfallen but
said nothing.

Uncle Yussef cried during the service. I don't remember ever
seeing him cry before – not even when my father died. He said
to me, 'It's like losing Selim again.'

George Conti and his wife came to the service. I would rather
they hadn't for, when I saw them, I couldn't help thinking that
they may be pleased. I'm becoming cruel.

At the cemetery, it seemed for a moment that the baby
would have to be buried in the Sahli crypt, in the neighboring
cemetery. The Greek Orthodox priests took exception to the fact
that the baby, baptized a Roman Catholic, was being buried in
a Greek Orthodox cemetery! Alexandre succeeded in mollifying
them. Now I wish he had not, then the baby would have been
buried with my mother and father, in the Greek Catholic
cemetery. I doubt that the Greek Catholic priests would have
raised a fuss.

I asked Alexandre and Gabrielle to let it be known I would
be receiving condolence visits only as of next week. Not now. I
want to see nobody now, talk to nobody.

September 18

Batta arrived this morning in tears. Om Batta is in Kasr al-Aini hospital with extensive burns to her chest, neck and right arm. Her face was spared. Her primus exploded last night while she was cooking. How awful! Could it have been self-inflicted? According to Batta, Hassan had been pestering his poor mother with incessant demands for money and had even stolen one of her gold bangles. No wonder she said that some children can destroy their parents. I told Batta to go ahead, that I would go to the hospital to see her mother, shortly. Alexandre put Batta in a cab. He offered to go to Kasr al-Aini in my stead. I got the feeling that he was uncomfortable at the thought that I would go for Om Batta when I did not go see little Yves.

My little Yves, who would have been about three weeks old by now. Simone does not know yet. She thinks he's still in the hospital.

September 19

Yesterday, Alexandre and Constance went to Kasr al-Aini – he in the morning, she in the evening – but they never managed to see Om Batta. They were apparently told that she is too unwell to be receiving visitors, and only her children may see her. I have a feeling that they saw her but don't want to tell me the terrible state she's in. They both said that the hospital is in a lamentable condition. I'll talk to Aristote as soon as he gets back. Perhaps we can have her transferred to the Greek hospital. I'll be going to Kasr al-Aini this afternoon. By myself. Then, if I have the courage, I'll go to the cemetery. To both cemeteries.

September 20

I arrived at Kasr al-Aini too late. Mahmud was at the hospital. He was beside himself. When I asked where Hassan was, he said, his voice trembling, 'If Hassan shows his face, I'll kill him.' He repeated that several times with such violence that I feared he might act on his threat. Batta tried to calm him. I told him that his mother would not want to hear him say such words. Batta's husband was nowhere to be seen, but many of Om Batta's neighbors were there.

If it was not an accident, how desperate Om Batta must have been. I wonder whether giving her some money the day she came to pay her condolences would have made a difference. I didn't think of it then. Mother was very fond of her.

Would the baby have been alive if Simone's paediatrician or Aristote had been around? I ask myself that question all the time. The hospital has yet to explain what exactly happened. I am afraid to ask but I must find out.

I have been thinking of a story my father used to tell us when we were little girls: the story of King Solomon's ring. It was meant to make the king happy when he was sad, and sad when he was happy. Inside the jeweler had inscribed the words: 'This too will pass.' It seems to me that this makes it all the worse. That such grief should pass.

Claire made no further journal entries.

* * *

On September 24, the newspapers reported a cholera outbreak in villages close to Cairo. Fears of a repeat of the decimating 1883 cholera epidemic spread throughout the country. For a moment, Egypt's fresh defeat at the United Nations over the Sudan question receded into the background. All the parties, factions and sects stood united in the face of the cholera, though there were the occasional whispers that, for the government, all this fuss about the disease, as well as the talk about the impending partition of Palestine, were providential diversions from its failure to secure for Egypt an honorable agreement with the British.

Bella Sahli joined a group of women on a tour of cholera-stricken villages. Iris and Gabrielle volunteered their services in hospitals in Cairo. Claire did not. She told Iris, 'I have had enough with death!' She would, however, join a team of women that sewed blankets for quick distribution to the hospitals.

The cholera outbreak was contained.

In November, Palestine was partitioned and there was more violence in the streets.

In December, Claire went to the cemetery for the first time since little Yves was buried. After that visit, she gave his crib and clothes to Batta, who was still hoping to get pregnant. She did ask Batta first, 'Are you sure you want these things?' meaning: 'Don't you fear that they might be an ill omen?' Batta insisted that she wanted the crib and the clothes.

1952: Nicolas

Nicolas Conti, Alexandre's younger brother, was an uncomplaining man. When his occasional heartburn became chronic and he began having bouts of nausea after meals, he avoided telling his sister Constance about it because she doted upon him like a mother, so he did not want to worry her. His wife Gabrielle, he did not tell at first because illness made her impatient; she was never ill. Upon finally admitting that he had a problem, he had minimized its severity.

Gabrielle loved him. He had no doubts about that. But she was neither tender nor nurturing. Even with their daughter Aida, she had few tender impulses. He was more the mother, the one eager to nurse Aida whenever she was ill, leaving work early to check on how she was doing and sitting by her bed late into the night.

Over the course of their eight years of married life, not only had Nicolas come to accept Gabrielle as she was, he had grown profoundly attached to her. She was stormy but, at the same time, solid and predictable, 'made all of a piece,' as Alexandre had observed soon after getting to know the two sisters. There were no uncertainties, no vacillations, no equivocations. Nicolas liked the fact that her face was an open book: you knew where you stood.

Within a couple of weeks of him taking her out to a dance, a bit on a whim but also because she had the reputation of being an exceptional dancer – that was a good ten years after Alexandre and Claire had eloped – she would make it clear to him that she wanted him for keeps, yet would tolerate no hard drinking, womanizing or even occasional gambling.

Initially, he had given her no grounds to believe that he would yield to her charm offensive, trumpeting his reluctance to settle down and give up his bachelor lifestyle. But she had pursued him with dogged determination, standing by his convertible, almost every morning, for him to give her a ride to work, then calling him, late at night, to ask him how he had spent his evening. It was her persistence that had, in the end, seduced him. She had made him feel enormously desired. He had realized that, underneath her independent, imperious exterior, she wanted an anchor, a man to lean on, and that realization would gradually awaken in him the desire to provide her with that anchor. At the age of forty-two, shortly before his internment during the war, he had proposed to her when she least expected it: just after she had reproached him with having paid too much attention to a mutual friend at a picnic.

Ready to relinquish his bachelor freedom, Nicolas dove into married life the way a pearl diver would into turbulent seas: with absolute faith and no hesitation. It was not in his nature to second-guess himself. And he had managed all right. They had managed all right. More than all right, he would say. Their strong physical attraction to one another did not dwindle. Marriage cemented it.

Like Gabrielle, Nicolas was stubborn and possessive though not mercurial. He kept his cool. He had squarish features and a strong jaw, was tall, broad-shouldered, muscular, swarthy without being suave. One imagined him to be most in his element outdoors. And so he was. He enjoyed hiking, shooting, sailing, cross-country motorcycling, playing a hard game of squash and pitching a tent. He had a practical bent of mind. He sang and danced beautifully, but spoke sparingly. Words were not his thing – neither words nor conversation, that was his brother Alexandre's domain. Eleven years apart, the two brothers shared only one characteristic: their height. Both were six feet. Fair and wiry, Alexandre had angular features. At ease in a salon, a café or a library, he was lost in front of any mechanical device and, though a great walker, not otherwise athletic. Even in their bad habits, the two brothers differed. Nicolas drank; Alexandre smoked.

Though so different in character and in their interests, the two brothers were loyal to one another and protective of each other. During Nicolas's hard-drinking days, Alexandre would tell his brother to drink less, but would silence similar criticism from anyone else. Whenever the subject of Alexandre's spendthrift ways cropped up, Nicolas would defend his brother, arguing that he spent more on others than on himself, his weakness was his generosity.

The loyalty between the two brothers would survive Nicolas's marriage to Gabrielle, by then an unrelenting critic of Alexandre. On the eve of the wedding, she had told Nicolas she had no patience for men like Alexandre, who were unable to provide their wives with material security and had pretensions exceeding what they could deliver.

Rather than argue with her, Nicolas had simply stated that he could not bear to hear his brother, of whom he was very fond, portrayed in such negative terms, that it hurt him, so could she please keep these thoughts to herself.

That Gabrielle harbored such negative feelings about his brother did not surprise Nicolas. She had worked hard from a young age, teaching science while studying law at the French

School of Law with the view to plead before the mixed courts; her rudimentary Arabic ruled out her arguing cases before the native courts. In 1937, the Montreux Treaty provided for the dissolution of the mixed courts, making her recently acquired degree worthless. The practice of law slipping through her fingers, she carried on teaching and acquired the reputation of being formidably strict and industrious. It was inevitable that Alexandre's checkered work history and volatile employer relations would irritate Gabrielle, who had worked steadily and conscientiously, doing something she had little passion for. Still, the vehemence of her remarks had disconcerted Nicolas. But he knew her to be extreme in her reactions, so he had put it down to her character.

Some years later, when, in a fit of exasperation, Alexandre had stomped out of Yussef Sahli's office, banging the door behind him, and the two men had fallen out for good, Nicolas would have grounds to question whether there was more to Gabrielle's hostility towards Alexandre. Upon hearing of the row, she had defended her uncle, saying, in Constance's presence, that Alexandre was quite impossible.

'Well Gabrielle, there was a time – it's true, a long time ago – when you did not find as many faults with Alexandre as you do now, or else I wouldn't have caught you once sitting on his lap,' Constance had interjected angrily, then had left the room just as Gabrielle was stammering, 'But ... but what ... what exactly are you implying?'

Nicolas had sought no clarifications, neither from Constance nor from Gabrielle. It was possible, he had silently concluded, that, early on in Alexandre's and Claire's marriage, Gabrielle had flirted with Alexandre. Possible too that their flirtation had ended on a rancorous note. Had Claire ever suspected her sister of flirting

– perhaps even more than flirting – with her husband? If she had, Nicolas was certain that, in keeping with her character, Claire would have said nothing.

Like most men, Nicolas admired Claire's looks. He found her beautiful but also unfathomable and too introspective for his liking. So quite apart from the fact that he had always seen her as his brother's wife and thus definitely off limits, he was not really touched by her beauty. He reckoned that a man would always be in a state of emotional uncertainty with a woman like her – a state in which he personally would loathe to be. He was the sort of man who, no matter the stakes, would rather lose than be confronted with an equivocal outcome.

Claire herself had few affinities with Nicolas. She judged him to be dull and too much of a man's man. But she did think well of him – not least because he was undaunted by Gabrielle. She might have grown to appreciate him more, had she got to know him better. However, the moment she had sensed that her sister was interested in him, knowing how possessive Gabrielle was, she had kept her distance. The last thing she wanted was to become Gabrielle's rival.

Told of Nicolas's health problems ('Only a bit of an ulcer,' he had said, omitting to add that the doctor was concerned), Constance and Alexandre immediately began worrying, while Gabrielle appeared almost indifferent, insisting that Nicolas was indestructible.

For a year or so, except for eliminating spices and liquor from his diet, Nicolas had gone about his life as usual. During that year, Constance would arrive at least twice a week at his place with special dishes she had prepared for him, leading Gabrielle to grumble that all this attention was bound to invite sickness.

At a party thrown by friends to usher in '52, Nicolas had sat for much of the evening, dancing only twice and only upon Gabrielle's insistence. That was unusual for him. At the party-goers' request, he sung an aria from *Aida*, at the end of which, heavily pregnant Claire, who had come without Alexandre, thought he seemed exhausted. She had gone up to him to ask him if he was all right. Sounding grateful that she should be inquiring, he assured her he was. 'Ah, there's Gabrielle dancing', he had observed wearily. While watching her sister swirl in the arms of one of Nicolas's friends, Claire found herself thinking a most unpleasant thought: should something happen to Nicolas, she would bear the brunt of her sister's sorrow. That thought – clear and frightening – had made her tell Nicolas, impulsively and in an intimate tone he was not accustomed to hearing her use, 'Please do look after yourself. You must!'

Nodding, he said, 'You too must look after yourself and you should start thinking of names for the baby. You hesitated so much over Djenane's name.' Two years after Yves's death, Claire had given birth to a baby girl and for two and a half weeks kept changing her mind about the baby's name. She started out naming her Ada, then decided she liked Ariane better, and eventually settled on Djenane.

'I have been thinking of names,' Claire said. 'A lot in fact, but that doesn't mean I'll find the decision any easier to make.' Nicolas smiled at her kindly.

* * *

Neither Claire nor Gabrielle was expecting Yussef Sahli to show up at the French hospital in Abbassiya where Nicolas had been rushed that morning.

It was a Monday afternoon. Cairenes were still shaken by the preceding week's events starting Friday in the city of Ismailiya. Suspecting it of collaborating in raids on their garrisons, British soldiers surrounded the Egyptian police force and enjoined the colonel in charge to lay down arms. The Wafdist Minister of Interior ordered his men to resist, so the British opened fire, slaughtering the police force. That night, the Egyptian government would break off diplomatic relations with Britain. The next morning, demonstrators, including policemen, students, Muslim Brothers and communists, would march to the Cabinet offices, demanding arms to fight the British in the Suez Canal. By around noon, a restless group of men had set fire to a cabaret in the heart of Cairo, their anger apparently ignited by the sight of a police officer drinking in the company of a dancer. Around the same time, the Rivoli, a nearby cinema, had gone up in flames; next, it was the Metro cinema; next, the Turf Club; next, Groppi's, and the Shepheard's Hotel, and Barclay's and the French Art Gallery, and Chrysler's, and large department stores but also smaller businesses as well as buildings on Suleiman Pasha, Kasr al-Nil, Malika Farida and Fuad Streets. By the end of the day, several hundred buildings had been destroyed or damaged. An unspecified number of people had died, including, in the Turf Club fire, the estranged British husband of one of Claire's friends.

After these tumultuous days, two questions were on everybody's mind: who was behind the burning of Cairo, and why had the army been sent to restore order in the city only late in the afternoon on Saturday?

Yussef Sahli was lucky. None of the buildings he owned was damaged. Saturday morning, on edge because of a business deal he was about to conclude, he had arrived at his office on Suleiman

Pasha Street at 7:30 A.M., earlier than usual. News of the trouble in the streets had reached him around midday. From then on, he would remain glued to the telephone, trying to ascertain whether it was safe for him to return to his home in Garden City.

Despite their dramatic falling out a couple of months earlier, he had called Alexandre, asking him, without so much as a 'hello,' to call immediately his close friend Maher, the son of an ex-prime minister, to find out what was going on.

Semi-flattered that Yussef Sahli should have thought of getting in touch with him, yet taking umbrage at his imperious tone, Alexandre had replied tersely that Maher was in fact about to pick him up as they were going to visit Nicolas who was feeling poorly; if there was any noteworthy news, he would try to call him back but not to count on it, for he had other things on his mind.

'And what's wrong with Nicolas?' Yussef had asked in a surly way.

'Surely you know that he has been suffering from ulcers,' Alexandre said, not hiding his indignation.

'A day like today would give ulcers to anybody,' Yussef shouted before hanging up.

* * *

Gathered in Nicolas's room, Gabrielle, Constance and Alexandre were waiting for the surgeon scheduled to operate on Nicolas the next day. Her lips pursed, her eyebrows arched, Constance sat on the edge of her chair. Alexandre and Gabrielle moved restlessly around the room. Claire alternated standing with sitting as her back was sore. The most relaxed-looking was Nicolas, though his olive complexion had a grayish tinge and his eyes were dim.

'Well, the good news is that the bank has not been damaged,' Claire was saying just as her uncle opened the door. Nicolas was a senior accountant at that bank.

'I admire you for trying to find some good news. Egypt's reputation is in shambles. Absolute shambles. We'll all pay a price, even those of us who have not suffered immediate losses.' Yussef growled while walking towards Nicolas's bedside.

As he passed Claire, he patted her cheek, 'You're huge,' he remarked, 'could it be twins?'

Standing by the bed, he asked Nicolas, 'And how is our patient?' then, turning towards Gabrielle, he said, grinning, 'I'm sure he can count on you not to overreact,' then, to Constance, he declared, 'Your brother is in good hands. The hospital has an excellent reputation.'

To Alexandre, he said nothing.

Yussef Sahli was, by that stage, a man in his late sixties, round, bald, almost always flustered, and made yet more frenetic and overbearing by the knowledge that stared him every day, right in the face, that he was on the downward slope of his business career, well past its pinnacle.

'So Gabrielle', he almost screamed, 'are you going to defend the rabble, as you did in '46 when they surrounded the British barracks?'

The regard in which Gabrielle held her uncle had not faded over the years. Her instinct was to avoid crossing swords with him. Still, on that subject, she was not willing to recant. She challenged him but tried not to sound antagonistic, 'But Uncle, in '46, the demonstrators were simply asking for their country's independence and were killed for that. They did not burn, they did not loot. You cannot compare the two situations.'

Yussef shrugged. For the first time since walking into the room, he looked at Alexandre, whom he asked brusquely, 'So what does your friend Maher have to say about this crazy business? Who was behind it? What does his father have to say? You never called me back.'

Alexandre took his time to answer before saying nonchalantly, 'Oh, his father is old and ailing and is no longer in the loop.'

'He was prime minister.' Yussef was exasperated.

'That was a long time ago,' Alexandre said.

'Well, what does Maher think?' Yussef shouted.

'Maher merely reported the rumors that the king and the British may have had something to do with what happened.'

Both Claire and Gabrielle quickly looked at Alexandre. Claire wondered whether he was trying to provoke her uncle, or whether he actually lent some credence to those rumors. Gabrielle, who was quite anti-British, wished Alexandre would say more but did not want to make that apparent; she never wanted to show too much interest in anything he had to say.

Yussef Sahli was neither for, nor against the British; neither for, nor against the king. He did not particularly mind the Muslim Brothers, perhaps because he did not take them seriously. Anti-communist, however, he definitely was. 'Nonsense,' he cried out. 'Unruly mobs manipulated by a bunch of opportunists. Communists I bet.'

Nicolas smiled.

Alexandre chuckled then said, 'Perhaps. Mind you, events like those have a way of turning people like us into ardent anti-nationalists, all to the benefit of the British and the king! Besides, there's no doubt that the Wafd has been enormously hurt by the turn of events. They're the main losers. They're out of power, and now the king thinks that he has the upper hand.'

'Leave the poor king out of that,' Constance told her brother. She felt allegiance to the royal family as the king's mother had been a neighbor of theirs when they were children.

'Your friend Maher is circulating the stupidest of rumors,' Yussef said. 'What would he know anyway? He paints but what else does he do? Absolutely nothing! I heard that he was planning on having an exhibition at the French Gallery. He was damn lucky that his paintings were not there when the gallery went up in flames.'

'First, he is not circulating rumors, merely reporting them,' Alexandre said. 'Besides, is it such a far-fetched theory? After all, it's very possible that the Greenshirts were behind what happened on Saturday. You must have heard that their top man, Ahmad Hussein, was seen downtown around noon on Saturday. It's common knowledge that he has been cozying up to the palace, getting money to stir the people against the Wafd. We cannot rule out the palace being behind some of this.'

Yussef shook his head and said with scorn, 'I'm sorry if I cannot understand the difference between circulating rumors and reporting them.' Then he looked at Claire and asked her, 'And you, what do you think? Or are you too pregnant to think?'

Alexandre frowned.

'On that score, you're right, Uncle. I am far too tired to think about anything,' Claire said.

'I think that we may be tiring Nicolas,' Constance said. 'Perhaps some of us ought to go to the visitors' room.'

'No need to,' Nicolas said, 'I'm fine.'

'I think that the British ...' Gabrielle began saying only to be interrupted by her uncle.

'Thoughts. Thoughts. Thoughts. It's facts we need, not thoughts,' Yussef said dismissively.

Gabrielle fell silent.

'Why don't you explain the events to us then?' Alexandre said.

'Uncle Yussef is right. All this speculation leads nowhere,' Gabrielle countered.

Vexed, Alexandre threw at her, 'But you yourself were about to offer us some theory.'

'Isn't it obvious what it was all about? As I said, mobs gone mad!' Yussef vociferated.

'But why did they go mad?' Alexandre said, his voice rising.

'Sorry to interrupt, but I'm getting a bit tired,' Nicolas said.

'What can I get you?' Constance immediately asked. 'Anything?'

'What he needs is peace of mind', Yussef said. 'Seeing the surgeon will give him that. As for me, I must be going. The driver is waiting.'

Before leaving, Yussef patted Nicolas's hand, saying, 'You'll be back shooting next week or the week after, unless they shoot us all in the meantime.' Then, he instructed Claire, 'Walk me to the car. Walking is good for you. Besides, I need to talk to you about Iris.'

Outside the room, Yussef asked Claire how Nicolas had taken the news that the small business in which he had invested some money had burnt to the ground. Claire was taken aback. 'What business?' she asked. She had no idea that Nicolas had invested money in a downtown business.

'You didn't know?' It was Yussef's turn to be surprised. 'You didn't know that he put a handsome little sum of money into a car repair shop as well as some of Constance's money? Against my advice, by the way.' He shook his head and went on, 'Well, you'd better say nothing. But let's talk about Iris and Anastase's plan to leave the country. Talk them out of it. Make them see the stupidity of it. Why leave family, friends, comfort, the country that has made you who you are? For what? They'll get no help from me whatsoever, if they go. None. You tell them that.'

Once in his car, Yussef called Claire to the window to say, with a slight quiver in his voice, 'Other than Anastase, you're the only one Iris listens to. You can influence her.' Then, quickly regaining his composure, he added sharply, 'I would think that you too would want to keep her in Cairo.' He sat back and then forward again as Claire began to walk away. 'And call me after you have talked to them,' he shouted after her.

When Claire returned to the room, Alexandre said, 'Your uncle was damn fortunate. Not so much as a spark touched his interests.'

'Well, thank God for that! Should we have wished otherwise?' Gabrielle asked pointedly.

'He has aged,' Claire said to deflect the train of the conversation.

'I'm actually quite tired now,' Nicolas said. 'If I could close my eyes for a few minutes that would be good.'

'Does he know what happened to the business he put his money in?' Claire asked herself. And, even more importantly, did Gabrielle know?

* * *

The operation, scheduled to take place around mid-morning the next day, was to last an hour at most, the French surgeon, newly arrived in Egypt, said when he dropped by in the evening. Out in the hallway, Claire managed to have a private conversation with him. 'Are you concerned, doctor?' she asked, thinking that he looked extremely young and self-assured.

'I'll be frank with you: more than I would like to be,' the doctor replied.

Claire's heart sank. The possibility that Nicolas might not make it frightened her. The feeling that Gabrielle would take it out on her returned. 'He seems so robust though,' she said to the doctor.

'Yes, he looks very robust,' the doctor agreed. 'We'll have to see though.'

When Gabrielle talked to the doctor, she avoided asking him how serious Nicolas's condition was. When he explained to her the surgical procedure that Nicolas would be undergoing, she listened without listening. She was squeamish about poor health and any related matters – a squeamishness that lay behind her apparent insensitivity to others' ailments.

Constance insisted on spending the night in the hospital. Gabrielle had to go back home to be with Aida.

In the course of the night, Nicolas told Constance about the burning down of the business in which he had sunk their money. Word of the destruction had come to him on Saturday evening. He said that the business was probably going to fold up anyway. The Frenchman who managed it, in whom he had put his trust, had been swindling him. She took the news with seeming unconcern and would not hear of the arrangements he had made for her to be compensated, should something happen to him.

Alexandre returned to the hospital in the very early hours, then, shortly afterwards, Gabrielle arrived, then Claire.

As scheduled, Nicolas was taken to the operating theater around mid-morning. Just before being wheeled there, while Gabrielle was bustling about, he whispered to Claire, 'I don't need to tell you how much you mean to Gabrielle, but I feel I must. Anything can happen.'

'Please, don't even think such thoughts,' Claire said.

An hour or so after Nicolas was taken away, Gabrielle, Alexandre and Constance began pacing up and down the hospital hallways.

Claire stayed in the room. She was reading when her Uncle Yussef called to find out how the operation had gone.

'He's still in the operating theater?' Yussef Sahli said in a surprised tone. 'I must confess that he doesn't look well at all. I didn't want to tell you that yesterday but I was really shocked by how poorly he looked. I hope it's nothing serious. The problems with the business in which he stupidly put his money would have definitely aggravated his condition.'

Two hours went by and still no news. An altercation between Gabrielle and Constance erupted. Constance wanted to look for the head nurse to check on what was going on in the operating room. 'Don't be ridiculous,' Gabrielle yelled at her sister-in-law.

Another hour elapsed. Alone again in Nicolas's room, Claire was suddenly hungry but felt too anxious to go to the cafeteria. Besides, she was expecting Iris and Bella to drop by any time. Her book no longer sustaining her interest, her mind wandered to Nicolas's statement that she 'meant so much to Gabrielle.'

What did he really mean? That she was to be forever subjected to the push and pull of Gabrielle's intense, but mixed feelings for her? That she would never break free from Gabrielle's envious admiration? Unwarranted as this admiration had become, since whatever advantage she may initially have had over her sister, her life was far from a brilliant success.

The surgeon suddenly appeared at the door, followed by an assistant. He looked exhausted, and not quite so young anymore.

'So, doctor?' Claire asked, struggling to get up under the weight of her pregnancy.

He came close to her while his assistant stayed behind, and without quite looking at her, he said, 'We did all we could. But it was far too far gone, even more so than I had feared.' Then, looking at her, he added, 'He was a very, very courageous man.'

'Please, don't leave me. Wait until Gabrielle returns. Please,' Claire said.

'Your sister is a strong woman. It will be hard, but she'll manage.'

'You must give her the news.'

'Of course. Now you sit down. I don't want you to get too upset. It would not be good in your condition.'

A few minutes later, when the surgeon told Gabrielle that Nicolas had died on the operating table, Gabrielle kept on saying, 'It was just an ulcer, just an ulcer.'

'And when I think that, all along, you treated him as if there was nothing the matter!' Constance screamed at her.

Ignoring Constance, Gabrielle turned towards Claire and let out angrily, 'It's all your fault. If it had not been for your stupid, stupid marriage ...' Realizing the enormity of what she had said, and what she was about to say, she stopped mid-sentence, casting a rapid glance at Alexandre – a glance that exuded despair and bitterness and loathing. After that, she slumped on the bed and broke down, tears streaming down her face.

Claire sat by her side and said softly, 'I'm sorry, Gabrielle, so sorry, so very sorry,' adding, almost inaudibly, 'for everything.'

Consumed by grief over his brother's unanticipated death, Alexandre told Claire the morning after, 'It should have been me – not him. I'm the older one,' and, in the same breath, he said, 'Your sister needed him; they were a couple, a real couple.'

* * *

Three days after Nicolas's funeral, Gabrielle was back at work, causing raised eyebrows among her family and friends. She functioned but was a bundle of nerves and lost weight. The expression on her face became perpetually angry. She decided to move out of the house she and Nicolas had bought in the suburbs. For several years after that, she would move with Aida from one furnished apartment to the next, with a regularity that seemed intended to convey that she had no home.

During the first three of those wandering years, Gabrielle would speak neither to Constance, who continued to blame her for Nicolas's death, nor to Alexandre, who took the position that he ought to be made Aida's co-guardian. Convinced that his claim to guardianship was just a means to gain control over their assets, Gabrielle refused to have anything to do with him.

She continued to see Claire, though barely concealed her bitterness at being the one to have lost a husband. Claire would learn to endure being the recipient of her constant criticism – its gist being that Claire lacked decisiveness, was too soft, could not confront problems head on and tended to bury her head in the sand. Paradoxically, critical as Gabrielle grew to be of Claire, no day went by without her calling to consult her sister about something – what book to read, which exhibition to see, or how to redecorate an apartment. Her growing disapproval of Claire seemed to be the flip side of an intense need to emulate her. The tension that grew between the two sisters following Nicolas's death – though the seeds were sown before his death – would never abate, even when, in her late fifties, Gabrielle would fall in love again.

Eventually, Gabrielle made up with Constance, enlisting her help to look after Aida. She also eventually made up with Alexandre, though forever reminding him that she considered him a failure.

In March 1952, two months after Nicolas's death, Claire gave birth to another girl. It took two weeks for her to choose a name – almost as long as it had for Djenane. This child began life as Nevine and ended up as Charlotte.

In July 1952, events that were initially described by Haydar Pasha, commander-in-chief of the Egyptian army, as a 'tempest in a teacup' would bring an end to the monarchy and the rise to power of a group of young men known as the Free Officers.

Constance lamented the passing of the monarchy.

Alexandre thought that the *coup d'état* might prove to be a good thing considering that General Naguib, the Free Officers' flag-bearer, talked about the need to create a truly cosmopolitan Egypt in which minorities would feel a legitimate part of the country.

Yussef Sahli decreed that it had saved Egypt from falling into communist hands.

Though still wrapped up in her sorrow, Gabrielle welcomed the prospect of Egypt achieving complete independence from the British.

And Claire? Claire admired the Free Officers' sagacity and their ability to effect a bloodless transition. She saw it as fitting, fair and timely that men with a middling to lower middle-class background should finally assume the reins of power. Yet, more than ever, she wished she were in a position to make a life for herself outside of

Egypt, as Iris and Anastase were about to. Her first day at work, in a recently inaugurated gallery of modern art owned by a friend of hers, happened to be July 26, 1952, the day King Faruq sailed into exile.

1962/63: Yussef

'We're not sure when the flight will leave. We're not even sure there will be a flight to Cairo today. We should know within the hour,' the Egypt Air attendant told Claire with undisguised impatience after which she closely inspected her nails, pushing the cuticles back.

'What's the problem?' Claire asked with apprehension.

'Crew problems, Madam. Problems over which we have no control.'

'But what do you mean "no control"? If the company has no control over the crew, then what does it have control over?'

'Madam, there's a problem with the crew. I know nothing else. Believe me, I wish I did, but I don't. So please, try to relax, find a seat and come back in half an hour.' Smiling – her first smile during that exchange – the attendant suggested, 'You're welcome to leave your suitcase here, if that makes it easier for you. I'll keep an eye on it.'

Claire seemed to hesitate.

'Don't worry! It will be here when you come back. I promise,' the attendant said with a robust laugh.

Beirut airport was small; there were few seats in its departure hall. Claire moved away from Egypt Air's counter, feeling lost. Her eyes were bothering her. She was still not used to wearing contact lenses. '*I should consider my six months' stay in Beirut more than worthwhile, if, by the time I leave, I can do without glasses*,' she had written to Gabrielle, soon after ordering the contact lenses. '*Yes, even if I don't end up accepting the job here*,' Claire had gone on, only to blot out that sentence, writing instead, '*Yes, even if nothing else comes of my stay here ... You know what I mean.*' Composing Egypt-bound letters was an exercise in elliptical writing, for fear that the Egyptian censor might take exception to the slightest hint of disloyalty to the country. On re-reading her letter and deciding that the censor had bigger fish to fry, she re-inserted the explicit reference to the job in Beirut.

Casting a glance around her in search of a seat, a bench, or somewhere to lean against, Claire despaired over her inability to tell whether she was relieved at the thought that she might not be on her way back to Cairo, or, on the contrary, upset by that prospect. She was in the same confused state she had sunk into after arriving in Beirut and that had kept her awake many a night: confused over whether to accept the job offer that had lured her there or return to her old job in Cairo.

In Beirut, she would have plenty of friends – Levantine Egyptians who had left Egypt once they realized they would run into difficulties under Nasser – but her salary would be meager, barely enough for her and her younger daughters to live on (Simone was already on her own, struggling in Europe). In Cairo, her social circle was dwindling but her job in the art gallery-turned-furniture store where she had been working since 1952 paid well, though she did not know how much longer she could count on it. The store's owner, a good friend of hers, was a wealthy man who had abandoned his assets in Egypt, as he believed that it was only a matter of time till the government seized them. He was now setting up shop in Beirut. 'Join me,' he kept telling Claire. 'You cannot count on your present situation in Egypt to last. The government will soon pounce on the store and once that happens, there's no predicting what will happen to you. You'll be like a hair in the soup.' Their friendship – that was what it was, no more – was such that he felt comfortable enough to be blunt with her: 'There are no prospects for a woman like you in today's Egypt. If you lose your job, you would be hard pressed to find anything else there, then what?' He knew that she had become the family's breadwinner, and was very fond of her. And because he saw she would be an asset to the new store, he was willing to keep the Beirut job offer open for a few months – enough time for her to make up her mind – but not indefinitely.

The choice confronting Claire was not just between relative comfort in Cairo for as long as it lasted and tight means in Beirut; or a life in which her milieu was vanishing and one rich in friendships. The choice involved more than money and lifestyle. It involved Alexandre, a man now in his seventies without the means to move to Beirut. Could she really leave him behind, emptying his life of the little bit he had left, namely, her presence, Djenane's and Charlotte's? On her Beirut salary, she could not support the three of them.

From Beirut, in a letter in which she was explaining to him that she would try out the job for a few months after which she would return to Cairo then have six more months to make up her mind, Claire had written:

The best thing about this decision is that it's not one! After six months in Cairo I'll need to make up my mind whether to return to Beirut or not. 'To be or not to be?' I suppose I should find it comforting that others before me suffered from indecisiveness, a condition which, in my case, grows worse by the day.

In her next letter to him, she wrote:

What frightens me is the significance of the decision facing me and its ramifications for all of us. Were you to live with Constance, it might be possible to sublet the apartment, in the hope that the rental income would allow you to come regularly to Beirut to see us. I think of you and the girls all the time. I miss home and all the familiar elements of my life in Cairo, notwithstanding the ever-increasing problems. The truth is that it is not easy to start again at my age and work the long hours we do here (R. is, as you know, a driven businessman). It is not easy to be subjected to the vagaries of authority, however benevolent that authority may be. As you must have guessed, I'm demoralized but tell myself I must resist self-pity. In our circumstances, emotions are a luxury we cannot afford. I must think of our future. To live, on a day-to-day basis, as I would in Cairo – my future there being so uncertain – strikes me, all of a sudden, as the worst possible solution. For all of us. But you tell me what you think. Please do, as you stand the most to lose, were I to relocate. I trust your ability to study the matter objectively.

Her tone hardened in a reply to a letter in which Alexandre said that he feared she had already made up her mind to leave Egypt, that he did not understand why she needed to spend more time in Beirut to assess the situation – a possibility she had broached with him. Her agitation discernible, she had written:

You're wrong. I have not made up my mind although I wish I had. Yes, I wish I had it in me to take the plunge. Wisdom and foresight would require I do, and that I put aside all the other problems which could be solved over time. Unfortunately, I am plagued with too vacillating a nature to make a decision – any decision – without immediately reconsidering it, be it buying a simple pair of shoes or moving house. You know me well enough to know that. I was hoping that you would help me overcome this crippling aspect of my character. I was asking for too much.

In a postscript, she had scribbled:

How I wish for some external factor to force a decision upon me, one way or the other!

A week after sending that letter, she received a telegram from Alexandre stating 'very ill uncle requests your presence.'

The telegram was followed by letters delivered by a friend of Claire's, who had just arrived in Beirut. In his letters – he had sent three – Alexandre was expressing the sentiment that, whatever his own personal feelings about the man, he thought she owed it to her uncle to be by his side at the end of his life. For her part, Gabrielle had written:

Uncle Yussef is not well. If you want to see him, you probably ought to come back sooner rather than later, but he might surprise us.

'I'll see what I can do,' Claire had telegraphed back. Suspecting Alexandre of using her uncle to precipitate her return, she avoided taking any step until a letter from Iris arrived:

You, of all people, know my ambivalent feelings towards my father. I'm sure you remember how, when I was little, I would tell anybody and everybody who cared to listen, 'I don't love Papa.' I was not trying to be singular! That was how I felt. Very early on in life, I sensed that I hardly existed for him. He had three children but only two really mattered to him. That's the truth. He chose to ignore me in almost all regards. My school successes counted for nothing. Never a 'well done;' never a 'bravo.' Not a single word of encouragement from him, not even when at the age of fifteen I entered an adult poetry competition. Nor one congratulatory word when I won it and my poem was published. No kudos either for doing six years of Latin in two years. All I would hear from him was criticism for being who I was coupled with implicit reproaches for being sick, as if I could have helped that! Need I go over that history again, his sending me, for my asthma, to a home that was actually an institution for people with mental problems? I was twenty-two at the time ... Why am I telling you all this, when you know it all?

Over the last couple of years, my feelings for him have changed somewhat. His reaction to the events in Egypt touched me. He has shown much less bitterness than I had anticipated. I was prepared to see him become even more egotistical, for which I would have excused him. After all, he has witnessed the death of the one real love of his life – the world of business. I sometimes think that the stroke he suffered a year ago was caused by those events. That he should have come out of his stroke relatively unimpaired is quite something for a man nearing eighty-five. That he should have come out of it a touch philosophical is the real miracle. He is infinitely more likeable now than when he had the world at his feet, don't you think? And yet, I cannot forget all the years during which he ignored me. Your presence, Claire, would be of immense help to me. There is something about you that pacifies me and brings out my better self (the little bit there is to bring out …). And he loves you very much. For those reasons, I need you in Cairo. It's very selfish of me to ask you to leave Beirut at this juncture. I know the predicament you're in. I know the anguish you're going through. I am sorry to be complicating your life. Forgive me.

My sweet Claire, come to Cairo so that we can be together in these difficult times. They're difficult both on a personal level and on a bigger scale. Cairo and Egypt are changing so fast that they will soon become unrecognizable to us. Will we ever get to the stage where they will be the mere shadow of a memory?

Your Iris

While waiting at the Egypt Air office in downtown Beirut for her ticket to be issued, two days after receiving Iris's letter, Claire would jot down on the margin of a newspaper, 'This every day we deemed to be so negligible and which we used to take for granted, how much we would like to revive it.'

* * *

The departure lounge began to fill. Standing in one corner, Claire had visions of jumping in a cab, returning to her pension and showing up for work the next morning.

Her thoughts then veered towards her daughters. She wondered whether her relative laissez-faire in raising her children had in fact harmed them more than helped them. She had let herself be guided by the principle that it was best not to force her children to do what they did not seem keen on doing. She had urged them to capitalize on their apparent strengths, encouraging the bookish one to read more books, the theatrical one to get on the stage and the beautiful one to tend to her good looks. This had backfired, certainly in the case of the older two who often accused her of having slotted them too readily into categories they were finding it hard to break out of. They felt she had given them a constraining view of themselves and their potential. In hindsight, she might have done it differently yet was not certain that the results would have been significantly different. In reality, Claire did not much believe in the virtues of education, if that meant the molding of characters. Teaching a child how to use cutlery properly, she was all for. But teaching a child what to think, how to think, what living life is about, she was less sure of. The only moral message she had ever tried to impart to her children was to avoid, to the extent possible, hurting people's feelings. One regret she definitely had. She blamed herself for allowing – even encouraging – Simone to leave Egypt and try her luck in Europe when she was not even twenty. Had she left to go to university, it would have been one thing, but it was work she was seeking as Claire did not have the means to support her in Europe. Having a vastly idealized concept of life in Europe, of the freedom this life would entail and the opportunities it would afford, she had not appreciated the difficulties Simone would face, the loneliness, the sense of isolation. 'She'll make it, if she wants to,' she had assumed, certain that where there is a will, there is bound to be some way. It had been, on her part, in part projection, in part identification with Simone's naïve enthusiasm and determination to go.

'I'll wait for another ten minutes after which if there's no sign the plane is departing, I'll head back to Beirut,' Claire suddenly decided while looking at her watch. When she looked up, she saw the Egypt Air employee waving in her direction. 'Damn, damn, damn!' she muttered under her breath and went to the counter to be told that the plane would be departing with a two-hour delay – 'only two hours,' the employee stated with jubilation as though it was news that should elate Claire. Then, pointing to a seat in the hall, the employee added, 'Here's an empty seat. You should grab it. You don't want to be standing for two hours.'

Claire was a fifty-two-year-old woman whom men, some even younger than her, still wooed. Her gray hair – more white in fact than salt and pepper – did not seem to have much dampened men's interest in her. As ever, they felt good in her company – both at ease and understood. Her features were still delicate, their purity still striking, her jaw line firm and face unlined. She had grown neither heavy nor thin; if her body was not quite youthful, her style of dress hid this well.

A man in her Beirut circle had fallen in love with her. However,

Beirut – not he – was on her mind as she took the empty seat spotted by the Egypt Air employee. Over the course of her six months in that city, she had come to enjoy its changeable weather, including the rain, wind and thunder – all so rare in Cairo – and even to take pleasure in climbing up and down its narrow, interlacing streets, hood on her head, clogs on her feet, wrapped up in a raincoat. At the beginning of her stay, the grocery stores and pastry shops used to overwhelm her. There was so much to buy. The displays were so inviting. In present-day Cairo, she had become accustomed to the rationing of meat, sugar, oil and the disappearance, from the grocery shelves, of most cheeses and cold cuts, of nuts and imported sweets, of any item that smacked of luxury. Beirut had struck her initially as a Cairo of the thirties and forties, though on a small scale and with a modern touch. She gradually revised her opinion. Beirut's café life in which men and women partook in equal measure gave it a languid, intimate atmosphere she had never experienced in Cairo, nor even in Alexandria. Together with the still very palpable French feel of the city, that atmosphere delighted her. Never having set foot there, Beirut's less Europeanized quarters – the poor Beirut – remained *terra incognita* for her. She imagined Beirut to be a city of sharp cleavages and divided worlds, although, based on her vague impressions, less so than Cairo. While there was a lot she did not know about Beirut, the little she knew, she liked a great deal. Could it be that Beirut's main attraction for her was providing her with a sense of liberation?

Checking her watch for the umpteenth time, Claire thought of her Uncle Yussef – whether his death would leave her sad, relieved or largely indifferent.

She was his favorite niece. Some said that she was the daughter he would have liked to have had. For several years – even after his falling out with Alexandre – he would call every morning around seven o'clock to tell her there was some important matter about which he needed her opinion, would she mind riding with him to the office, the driver would take her back home after dropping him off. During those years, which ended only once he started suffering from poor health and took to staying at home, it became part of her daily routine to accompany him to his office – a trip that lasted between five to eight minutes, depending on the traffic lights. He would rarely solicit her opinion. He never much solicited anyone's opinion. He simply wanted her company and the opportunity to give vent to whatever happened to be bothering him that day as plenty used to bother him; agitation seemed to be his second nature.

Had there been more to his affection than the attachment of an uncle to a preferred niece? Every so often that possibility would cross Claire's mind without arousing anger since there had never been any transgression on his part.

A month after her father's funeral, they had had their first confrontation. He was hoping to dissuade her from sitting for the *bac*, saying it was more trouble than it was worth, and the nuns at her school had better things to do than to cater to her whims. She would not yield. Nonplussed by the firmness of her resolve and her composure, he had let her be that time – not that there was much he could have done to stand in her way since she had already won over the nuns.

Barely a couple of years after that little skirmish, their big war would erupt. On hearing her announce to him that she was smitten by Alexandre, a good friend of his, and that they were considering getting engaged, he had yelled, the veins of his throat swelling so much that she had grown alarmed, 'You're thinking of getting engaged to him? An impractical squanderer twice your age? You're barely seventeen! Over my dead body, you hear! Over my dead body.' But she would not capitulate and, with remarkable sang-froid, had proceeded to enumerate Alexandre's virtues, many more than she had been aware of before her uncle's outburst. They had fought for almost two years – Yussef alternating threats with pleas. When she married Alexandre, he crossed her off his life. Even Gabrielle was forbidden to make mention of her sister in his presence. Then, some ten years later, he had bumped into her at a party and all was forgiven. Not only had he welcomed her back into his life but he had welcomed Alexandre too, insisting they work together. By way of a reconciliation and belated wedding present, he had given them an apartment to be furnished to their taste, at his expense.

Shortly after her thirtieth birthday, they were again at loggerheads. This time it was over her wanting to leave Alexandre for Guy. The intensity of his reaction at the prospect that she might be leaving the country with a man she had fallen in love with had been so excessive, his hostility towards Guy, whom he had never met, so visceral, that she did wonder about the nature of his feelings for her. He had reacted as if he and not Alexandre was the one about to be jilted, arguing Alexandre's case as though arguing his own.

Out of her adolescent confrontations with her uncle, Claire had emerged victorious. Out of that episode, he had, since she would give up Guy. At the time, Claire had resented her uncle enormously for the pressure he had brought to bear upon her, including issuing an order to his daughters Bella and Iris to cut off all contact with her – an order both girls ignored, calling her right away to express their solidarity. 'To hell with him. We're with you all the way,' Bella had said.

Brooding over these episodes in her life, Claire found herself now begrudging her uncle more his stand when she was a sixteen-year-old girl in love with Alexandre than his subsequent opposition to her wanting to end her marriage. In retrospect, it seemed to her that it was her uncle's heavy-handedness that had precipitated her marriage, that his disapproval – he who stood for much of what she then derided, namely, unabashed materialism – had solidified her resolve. Had he been less vituperative, her infatuation might have run its course, and Alexandre might not have felt as honor-bound to stick to his probably impulsive proposal that they get engaged. Her uncle might have been able to talk her out of getting married by offering to send her to France to do a degree in philosophy. But there had been no such offer – not even a hint of it. As she now saw it, besides being instrumental in her decision to stay with Alexandre – an arrangement that would suit him, making her more available to him than had she remade a life with another man – he was to some extent responsible for her marrying as young as she had, as foolishly as she had.

It was too late for her to tell him any of this. As it was too late for her to ask him why her father, a successful lawyer, died leaving so few assets. Had her uncle really been their savior, moving the family into an apartment he owned to save them additional expenses in view of their reduced circumstances? Or had he appropriated her father's assets, her mother being in no position to defend herself?

There are moments in one's life when one sees oneself in a new light. Sometimes, that fresh aspect is consistent with the overall picture one has of oneself, sometimes not. Young, Claire had not been interested in the material side of things. She would not have married Alexandre otherwise; would not have been about to turn her life upside down for Guy, a young man without money; would not have rejected, at the age of thirty-five, the advances of one of Egypt's wealthiest men known for the munificent presents he lavished on his mistresses. She had worn her relative lack of means with appealing unconcern, sewing her own gown for the *Bal des Petits Lits Blancs* in 1944 – a particularly grand occasion – without feeling hard-done-by. Her concern about money surfaced as she approached fifty, which also happened to be the time when, thanks to Nasser, her world began to disintegrate. That concern was becoming more than just concern, bitterness was taking hold of her. A bitterness that was making her question her uncle's integrity – whether he had been honest in his dealings with her, Gabrielle and their mother – as well as almost regret the many hours she had spent over the years lending him an attentive ear since not a piaster from his estate would she inherit. While waiting to board her plane, acutely aware of and distressed by the depth of her resentments – bitter at being bitter – Claire reckoned that she ought to have attached importance to money when she was young, she would have been all round – even morally – better off for it. 'Disillusionment with oneself is harder than disillusionment with others,' was her next thought.

The irony that she should cast such a negative eye on her uncle just as her cousin Iris was beginning to see virtues in him did not escape her. Iris was attributing her father's relatively serene acceptance of events in Egypt to a laudable transformation in his character. Claire had a different take on it. His affairs had started to flag before Nasser. Age had dulled his business instinct. He would have felt some relief at no longer having to put his business acumen to the test – hence, his philosophical stance. Besides, he had not been as affected as many others in Egypt's wealthy class. Not yet, in any case. Yes, the agrarian reform had hit him hard and he had lost a great deal of money on the stock market following the government's freeze of that market. But the bulk of his assets – the real estate he owned – had not been touched. There were rumors he was being protected by a political intelligence service agent, the son of his office handyman. All in all, he had been relatively fortunate. He would have been better off to get his money out of the country before the government restrictions came into force, but he had lacked that foresight. His assessment of the situation had been poor. Very poor.

When, soon after the 1952 coup, the military junta passed a decree limiting the ownership of agricultural land, Yussef Sahli insisted that the agricultural reform should not be taken as a signal of more threatening changes elsewhere.

Two years later, he shrugged off General Naguib's removal from the presidency, his confinement to house arrest and the fading of any hope for a civilian government. He chose to believe the allegations implicating General Naguib in an attempt by elements of the Muslim Brotherhood to assassinate Nasser. 'We should take it as a good sign that the Americans seem favorable to Nasser. They understand that Egypt is not ready for democracy,' was his line. He was a touch troubled however by news of the death in jail, during the mass arrests of Muslim Brothers, of Om Batta's son Mahmud, whom he had known as a child. It troubled him less to hear of the imprisonment, for communist activities, of the son of Alexandre's friend, Maher. 'Why was the grandson of an ex-prime minister consorting with communists?' was all he had to say about the incarceration of the young man for joining a reading group eager to decipher *Das Kapital*.

In 1956, nationalist sentiments – somewhat out of character – put him squarely in Nasser's camp. He was all for the nationalization of the Suez Canal, and incensed at the tripartite aggression, going so far as to declare Nasser a great man.

Six months later, the process of 'Egyptianization' of the economy would give him some cause for concern. So would the sequestration of the assets of some of his friends, Egyptian Jews. Yet, to his son-in-law Anastase who, from Switzerland, was urging him to leave Egypt, he wrote at the time:

> *It's premature; let's not rush to any conclusion; after all, we have just come out of a war; it will take a little while for tempers to simmer down, but I'm sure they will in due course.*

Towards the end of 1957, when Nasser began talking of socialism, Yussef said to his entourage, 'These are words! Only words! Nasser wants and needs the Americans. He cannot abide the communists. Sure, he has been buying arms from the Soviet Union but only because he had to.'

In 1958, he whole-heartedly applauded Egypt's union with Syria, seeing in it solid business opportunities for the two countries.

In 1959, Nasser's rift with Khrushchev over events in Iraq, where the communists were helping crush Arab nationalists in Mosul and Kirkuk, seemed to vindicate him. 'Didn't I tell you that Nasser is no socialist! He's too smart to go down that path. He's got nothing to gain from asphyxiating the private sector.' America's closer ties with Egypt in the late 1950s would, in his eyes, confirm this.

'But why, why?' he shouted, in February 1960, on hearing of

the nationalization of Egypt's two main banks. A couple of months later, in the wake of the nationalization of the press, he said, 'I'm too old to leave the country, let's see what happens next.' Next he suffered the stroke from which he would fully recover despite his age. 'Do me a favor,' he told his wife after coming round, 'don't attribute my health problems to what's happening in the country! I don't want to hear that.'

In the early 1960s, with the government taking over all of Egypt's import trade, much of its export trade, as well as banks, insurance companies, and industrial and commercial businesses, there was no more room for speculation, for 'whys and wherefores.' Another round of nationalizations coupled with the sequestration of the properties of hundreds of Egypt's wealthiest families – those under sequestration were forbidden to participate in the country's political life – came on the heels of Syria's secession from its union with Egypt. It would be during that period – the fall of 1961 and early winter of 1962 – that Yussef Sahli finally understood he was living in a different world. What would bring this home to him was a political event: the jailing in Cairo of a young French diplomat whom he had befriended. Together with three colleagues, the young man stood accused of spying and was brought to trial only to be released with his colleagues, before the trial ended, just around the time the French government freed Ben Bella and it became apparent that Algeria was nearing independence. 'I guess the rules of the game have changed,' her uncle said to Claire one morning as they were driving to the tribunal to attend a hearing. That was before the young man's release. 'Your father would undoubtedly have had a theory to explain all this to us – a sensible, even-handed theory I'm sure. As far as I'm concerned, Egypt has gone to pieces, but perhaps I'm being too self-referential,' he added wistfully. Never before had Claire heard her uncle express himself with anything less than absolute certainty or engage in the slightest form of self-criticism.

'Am I judging him too harshly?' Claire asked herself, as she heard the boarding call.

* * *

Yussef Sahli was conscious when Claire entered his room. She was no longer angry with him. She was just very weary.

'So you're back!' her uncle said. 'I'm glad.'

'How are you feeling, Uncle Yussef?'

'Not well,' he said, 'Not well, but that's normal. I'm about to turn eighty-five. Remember?'

'We'll have to celebrate,' she said.

'It's not your style to utter platitudes,' he said then asked, 'Are you going back to Beirut?'

'I don't know,' she said, then repeated, 'I don't know.'

He closed his eyes.

She looked away. The smallest details of the events leading to her son's death came back to her. Thoughts of her father dying came back to her too. Her eyes filled with tears, something that seldom happened. She heard her uncle say, 'Your problem in life is that you are too lovable, too gentle.'

'I won't disabuse him,' she thought, instead smiling feebly at him.

'Be careful,' he said, his tone becoming agitated. 'If you go back to Beirut, your Aunt Farida and Bella might ask you to smuggle jewelry out of the country, to hide some in the hem of your dress. Don't, even if they offer you something in return!'

Wondering what would be on offer – her uncle's wife had magnificent pieces of jewelry, including a ruby necklace worth a small fortune – Claire told him not to worry. 'I don't think that I would have the courage, Uncle, so don't lose any sleep over it,' she said.

'Good,' he said and relaxed. 'But you're wrong. Courage you have, though not of the right sort.'

He died a week later, on the eve of his birthday.

The issue of the jewelry to be smuggled out of Egypt did not come up. Claire ended up staying in Cairo, almost by default. She could not make up her mind to leave.

1968: Alexandre

'Frankly, Madam, you're an embarrassment to the corporation. Not only are you being paid for doing virtually nothing – with your lamentable Arabic you're incapable of doing much of anything – but you get paid a lot, a huge amount to do the little you do. It's an intolerable situation. Management can no longer put up with it. They can no longer make allowances for your ineffective presence in the store. It was clear from the moment the store was nationalized last year that something would have to be done. Management has been ultra-patient, you must admit. But we reached the point where something needed to be done.' Claire's immediate supervisor, a burly man who reeked of cologne and wore sunglasses indoors, spoke slowly as if he was uncertain whether Claire understood him. Puffing on his cigarette with a weary air, he went on, 'At a meeting yesterday, it was decided that the time has come to solve the problem, so a decision was made to transfer you to a branch in Minya.'

'Minya?'

'Yes, yes, Minya! Starting the first of next month,' he said casually, as though speaking of a routine occurrence.

'But I have an elderly husband who is not well and a daughter who is sixteen years old,' Claire said without disclosing the fact that her daughter was about to go to Germany on a scholarship.

For a split second, her supervisor seemed uneasy. He fidgeted on his chair. 'Well, take them with you,' he said. 'Take them with you.'

'I don't understand,' Claire said bewildered and, drawing on her best Arabic, argued, 'The fact that I speak French and English is of some use, here. More so than in Minya. Here, my salary is not so out of line with other employees' salaries. I can even think of one person whose salary is higher than mine. In Minya, salaries must be much lower than in Cairo. Won't I be even more of an embarrassment to the corporation there? I really don't understand.'

'First, I don't see how you can compare yourself to *Ustaz* Hamdi, as it's him you must be referring to. He reads and writes Arabic. There's no mistaking *him* for a *Khawaga*. But the point is that we're not forcing you to go to Minya. Far from it! Whether you want to keep working is entirely up to you.'

'If I stop, I wouldn't get much of a pension. I am fifty-eight years old,' Claire said, with as much calm as she could muster.

'I cannot make that decision for you. I called you to my office to communicate to you the decision management made yesterday. I'm sorry but your family problems are yours, not theirs. You have almost a month to look after your family affairs, which is not bad. We could have ordered your immediate transfer and insisted you be in Minya within three days. I am not sure you realize this. You're working in the public sector now. What more can I tell you?' The supervisor got up hastily, walked to the doorway and yelled down the hallway, 'Ahmad, have you forgotten my afternoon cup of coffee? I need it badly. I'm getting a headache.'

For once not overcome by her usual indecisiveness, Claire walked out of that meeting determined to go to Minya and see a lawyer. She wasn't in a position to quit eighteen months away from her pension. It was clear to her that the management had come up with the Minya idea to force her to do so; under the new labor laws they could not fire her.

She would stick to her resolution and go to Minya, a city about 155 miles south of Cairo, where she worked for eighteen months in a store that sold an odd assortment of items – from ladies' underwear to light fixtures and home appliances but also copy-books, pencils and erasers. And she retained the services of a leftist lawyer, Hamid Hassanein, the son of Alexandre's friend Maher and grandson of an ex-prime minister, whose family had owned huge tracts of land in the Delta before the agrarian reform. In between stints in jail for communist activities, despite his halting speech and unprepossessing countenance, the young man was making a name for himself as a labor lawyer willing to take on hard cases. He was rumored to have been involved in organizing the worker–student demonstrations held in February of that year – the largest Egypt had seen since 1954 – in which a crowd stretched out over a mile-long path had wound its way from Cairo University to the *Maglis-al-Umma*, demanding elections and an end to the police state. The lenient sentences received by Egypt's top officers for their mishandling of the June 1967 war had sparked the demonstrations as well as heated debates about what had gone wrong for the country to have suffered such a crushing defeat. Was the single-party system to blame? Had God inflicted that punishment on Egyptians for embracing socialism, a departure from Islam, or had the problem been insufficient socialism? Was it, more simply, the case of the men in charge being corrupt and self-seeking – Nasser himself, however, remaining unassailable? Elements from all walks of Egypt's political life – the Muslim Brotherhood, the liberal center, and the left – had participated in the February demonstrations, with the left playing the biggest role.

Claire did not hold his political activism against Hamid Hassanein. Quite the contrary, she thought it spoke well of the man. She had difficulties though imagining him in a political context because he was so self-effacing, which made her think all the more highly of him. He took on her case without requesting she pay him anything. 'Don't worry,' he told her, 'let's see whether we get anywhere, we can discuss my fees later.' He also told her, from the outset, that he was doubtful the transfer decision could be reversed, though he would give it a try. His main objective would be to protect her pension entitlement and ensure its proper calculation as he feared that the corporation's management would, when the time came, try to do her out of some of it. He was right. The court dealing with Claire's transfer to Minya upheld the transfer. Then, when Claire retired at age sixty, the corporation undervalued her pension. A court case that lasted for six years would in the end be decided in her favor. During those six years, Hamid Hassanein spent time in jail intermittently on account of his political activities.

* * *

The evening after being told of her transfer to Minya, Claire went to play bridge at a friend's place.

'You're going to Minya?' her friends asked in shock. 'Years ago, Minya may have been alright. Several big landowners used to have second homes there. It also had a large Greek community. But now the city is dead. Completely dead. And if one does not like the heat – you certainly don't – it's uninhabitable in the summer. Are you really serious about going?' one of them asked point blank.

'Yes,' Claire said while trying to concentrate on the game. Usually, she kept her problems to herself but had made an exception that evening which she was now regretting.

'It's an extremely courageous thing to do,' her bridge partner said.

'Courage presupposes some choice. I don't see myself as having a real choice in the matter,' Claire said, suppressing her growing irritation at the unhelpful remarks.

'It's monstrous on their part to be doing that, knowing how totally unsuitable the position and the city are for a person like you.'

'I suppose that's the point they're trying to make. Is it not?' Laughing an artificial laugh, Claire added, 'They decided to put me through a mini cultural revolution. I guess that's it.'

'But Claire, are you being realistic about your ability to cope with life there? You'll be working in a store that sounds like a hole, surrounded by people with such a different mentality,' her hostess asked while circulating snacks.

'With enough books, and if I find a few bridge partners, the time will pass.'

'You might find bridge partners at the Greek Club, if it still exists. But do you think it wise to consult Maher's son? I would be nervous. He has two strikes against him. He is *ancien régime* and apparently a communist – quite a combination. Did you know that he has been in jail?'

'My inclination is to trust a man who has been in jail for his convictions.'

'Well and good, but won't the judges hold that against him?' Gabrielle, also invited, said.

'I was told that his practice has been growing so he must be winning some cases,' Claire said.

'Let's hope he manages to keep you in Cairo,' the hostess chimed in. She knew of the tensions between the two sisters.

'If I win tonight, I'll take it as an auspicious sign,' Claire thought.

She lost.

On her way home in a cab – she had left with Gabrielle whose car was being repaired – she went over the game, concluding that two of her bids had been poor.

'Stop worrying about it,' Gabrielle advised her. 'You have bigger problems.'

'Oh, stop, Gabrielle. Stop!' Claire cried out with an intensity that suggested she may have been close to one of her rare outbursts. 'Why is everyone so keen on highlighting the difficulties I'll be facing?'

'All right, all right,' Gabrielle exclaimed and backed off. Usually the one to make scenes, she would be thrown off balance the few times Claire did, or seemed about to. Gabrielle was about to ask Claire how Alexandre, who had had two small strokes in the course of the year, was taking the news but thought better of it.

As if she had read Gabrielle's mind, Claire – now calmer – said, 'Alexandre will be moving in with Constance. It won't be the first time.' She was referring to the year he had spent at Constance's, ten years earlier, after a major row brought on by an affair she was having at the time.

'So he knows,' Gabrielle said.

'Not yet, but I talked to Constance.'

'What did she have to say?'

Claire shrugged. 'What do you expect her to say? "No" after all these years of self-sacrifice?' After a brief pause, Claire added, 'Batta and her daughter will be helping her. I made the necessary arrangements.'

* * *

Alexandre's custom was to send his letters express, no matter their contents. In keeping with that habit, his handwriting was bold and hurried-looking.

Just over two weeks after her arrival in Minya, the elderly doorman of the small hotel in which she was renting a room handed Claire such a letter. She had just stepped into the hotel bathed in perspiration. It was 1:30 P.M. The temperature was almost 44 degrees Celsius – not uncommon in Minya in August. Claire set the envelope on a rickety hallway table. Like most of the city's buildings with past grandeur, the hotel had a dilapidated look. She closed her parasol and got a fan out of her handbag.

'Sit down, sit down,' the doorman urged her, moving a shabby armchair closer to where she stood. 'I'll get you a glass of ice water.'

'Thank you, thank you, don't bother with the water,' Claire said, frowning as she glanced at the envelope. The letter was from Constance, not Alexandre – she could tell from the handwriting – and that alarmed her.

Alexandre had had another minor stroke. For two days, he had been thoroughly confused, mistaking Constance for her, and his own reflection in the large mirror hanging in his room for his brother Nicolas. As on the previous occasions when he had suffered from minor strokes, the confusion went away but he was left feeling feeble and, though lucid, was irritable, wanting company almost all the time. The doctor said that his irritability should pass but his wanting company might not.

'Not bad news, I hope,' the doorman said.

'In truth, not so good,' Claire said and asked him how she could place a call to Cairo.

'Don't you worry,' he assured her. 'I'll look after this for you. I'll go to the telephone company and book a time for tonight, after you come back from work. How would that be?'

'That would be really good,' she said as she got up to go to her room. She had planned on dropping in at the Greek Club after work for a bridge game. It was the prospect of that outing that had kept her going the last couple of days. As she climbed the hotel's dusty staircase with leaden steps, she brooded upon the unpleasantness she had been put through at work since her arrival, and had a sinking feeling there was more of it to come.

The first thing she did upon entering her room was to switch on the big electric fan she had bought the day after her arrival, moving it as close to her bed as possible. Next, she half lay on the bed, her back against the wall, her hand resting on her damp forehead. She undid the buttons of her blouse but felt too tired to get out of her clothes, too tired to reach for the copybook on the bedside table in which, to let off steam, she had made it a habit to keep a record of her troubles at work and chronicle the events of the day.

'What shall I tell Constance? What can I tell her?' Claire wondered. Then the inevitable regret, 'Why, oh why, didn't I stay in Beirut when I had the opportunity?'

* * *

Claire's salary was public knowledge in the Minya store before she set foot in it. On her first morning at work, a little girl no older than ten – the relative of one of the store's six employees, in the store with her mother to get herself a birthday dress – kept staring at Claire and eventually, just before leaving, said to her giggling, 'Can I ask you a secret question?' 'Sure,' Claire replied. The little girl whispered in her ear, 'Is it true that you're earning much, much more money than anybody else in the store except for the director? Ten times more?' Later that morning, when the shop assistant's helper complained of a toothache, one of the four shop assistants suggested loudly, 'Well, if you need Rivos, I'm sure that Madam can afford buying you some. Madam could afford buying you a lifetime supply of Rivos.' Except for the one woman shop assistant – a young woman called Mona – all the assistants on the floor burst out laughing. Where things stood could not have been clearer. Mona would become Claire's protector in the store, whereas the men, some more systematically than others, would take turns making life unpleasant for her. Within a week of her arrival, a couple of them would tell her in private that their actions did not reflect their true feelings but they feared the repercussions of showing her any sympathy.

Each employee had a chair on which they were authorized to sit when they had no customers. On her second day at work, Claire's chair disappeared several times in the course of the morning. 'Can't you take a bit of a joke?' the culprit said when she finally showed her exasperation.

The third day, an electric fan standing close to her Women's Wear Department was moved away on the pretext that hers was the cooler part of the store. Then, her fly swatter went missing. 'Madam needs a chair, a fan, a fly swatter. But we're here to work. Maybe Madam does not realize this,' the shop assistant in charge of home appliances said, not an ounce of levity in his tone. He did not even try to pretend he was joking. Later that day, hunting for her chair – she needed to sit to tack the hem of a dress a customer was trying on – the man declared for all to hear, 'But if she cannot kneel to do the job, isn't it time for her to retire?' causing Mona to exclaim, also for all to hear, 'Enough nonsense;' words that had on Claire the effect of a most precious balm.

On the fifth day, there was a lull, although shortly before closing time her persecutors' ringleader, the assistant in charge of home appliances, raised, out of the blue, the subject of the 1967 war. Looking in her direction, he asserted that the *Khawagas* in the country were either indifferent to what that defeat really meant for Egypt and the Arab world, or, even worse, secretly happy at the terrible outcome. And, hadn't they, in all likelihood, rejoiced the day Nasser announced his resignation only to bemoan his subsequent decision to stay on in response to popular support, the sales assistant asked, clearly rhetorically. Claire chose to ignore these remarks, in part because she would have found it difficult to express her views persuasively on such matters in Arabic. Besides, the man was unlikely to believe that she felt as strongly for the Palestinian cause as she did. So what would have been the point?

Mention of the *Khawagas* in the country in that derogatory tone was to become a frequent occurrence after that, particularly when some of the few remaining members of the Greek and Syro-Lebanese communities of Minya began dropping in, sometimes to buy something but other times just to chat with Claire. 'Madam thinks that the store is a club,' one or the other of the shop assistants would mutter. She pretended not to hear.

Her second week at work started with her being told by two of the shop assistants that, from now on, she would have to walk the goods bought in her department over to the counter where they were wrapped, as the shop assistants' helper was too busy to lend her a hand. 'But he is doing that for everyone else!' she objected and went to complain to the store's director, who hardly ever came out of his back office. He commiserated with her, saying that he wished he could help her but this was Upper Egypt, where outsiders were never much welcome, as he himself, being from Alexandria, had unfortunately experienced. The following morning, he called her to his office with an offer he would have to run by top management in Cairo: would she consider the position of *Mufatescha* – a supervisory position that might secure her the respect of her co-employees? It would involve her filling him in on all that was happening and being said in the store. She declined, invoking her bad Arabic. 'But you don't need to say much, just to listen to what is being said,' the director countered. She agreed to mull it over, knowing that she would not accept, even assuming the offer was serious. The job's duties went against her nature. Besides, the offer smacked of a trap: a supervisory role would likely exacerbate, not curb, the employees' hostility towards her. 'I cannot force you,' the director said on hearing her final decision, after which he made her another, most incongruous, offer. He was thinking of borrowing money from the bank for which he needed a guarantor. If she were willing to act as his guarantor, he would act as hers. 'But I'm not thinking of taking a loan,' she said weakly, as she had no wish to alienate him. 'Think about it,' he said with an unctuous smile. 'You never know. At some point, you might well need some extra money so it would be a mutually beneficial arrangement.' She left his office cursing herself for having gone to see him in the first place.

That very same day, a sales assistant in trouble for the disappearance of a couple of watches went up to her and said angrily, 'I'm a dangerous man, you know. I am capable of doing much harm, of hurting people. I thought I should let you know that.' His threats – he looked fierce as he uttered them – left Claire in a state of consternation. Had he got wind of the director's idea of giving her a supervisory role in the store, and had this been his way of warning her that she would be well-advised never to make an unfavorable report about him? She had been thinking in fact of offering him some money, to help him with the fine for the vanished watches. His threat made it impossible for her to make the offer.

On her return to her hotel room that day, Claire would write in her copybook:

> *The staff hold me responsible for their poverty; they compare their lot to mine and don't see me as a victim. They see me as a very privileged person, whose presence in the store is an affront to them. I can understand them. I would have felt the way they do. Would I have reacted as they have? I don't know. I don't fault them. I fault management 100 percent. Those in charge put me in a hopeless situation while giving the store employees yet more reasons to be unhappy with their lot. They have failed in their duties as managers since I will not resign and, although they have managed to sow the seeds of hatred towards me, I'm sure they have sown them towards the corporation too. I don't know what turn events will take, but should something happen to me, management and only management would be the guilty party.*

Then, in a postscript, she had added:

*Work gives man a feeling of self-worth. It connects him to
society.*

And in a second postscript:

*Mona has asked me to teach her French. I have agreed. I'll spend
a couple of hours a week doing that. On Sunday morning and
maybe once a week after work. In my hotel room. She is a very
bright young woman. I have a feeling that she will learn fast.
Thinking of the difficulties she is facing in life – having to give
her meager salary to her father to help support eight children
whom she has been mothering since her own mother's death –
should reconcile me to the difficulties I am facing. I have decided
to brush up my English by reading* The Forsyte Saga.

* * *

Still feeling the effect of getting from the store to the hotel – barely
ten minutes walk but much of it in direct sun – Claire remembered
that Alexandre's seventy-ninth birthday was in two weeks' time.
He was thirty-seven when they first met, and thirty-nine when
they married.

If he truly loved her, he would have let go of her a long time ago
and urged her to remake her life instead of hanging on to her, she
thought, not for the first time.

'The nonentity I have become,' was how he had described
himself the day after his sixty-ninth birthday, in a letter asking
her to consider a reconciliation. At the time – he had moved in
with Constance – his use of that epithet had filled her with a
compassion so strong that she had, at once, agreed to meet him for

a beer at Groppi's – a meeting that would lead, after several more, to his return home. Now his describing himself in those terrible terms seemed to her more a ploy aimed at softening her than a cry from the heart. In truth though, it was not just his holding on to her that had kept her locked in the marriage. With her sense of fair play, how could she have abandoned him, once she had foisted on him children that may not have been his; children whom he, no matter what he may have suspected, had accepted as his, be it out of pride, in self-delusion, or as a way to keep her? She had wanted children from early on in the marriage, yet, by thirty, still had none. After Guy, her desire for children had become all consuming, much exceeding her desire for love. She would gradually come to see her marriage as affording her the possibility of having children, no matter whose they were. That was how she had come to terms with it. And perhaps the children were his. Paradoxically, she might have found it easier to leave him, had she been certain that he was their father. She would have felt she owed him less.

When, after several attempts, Claire managed that evening to place her telephone call to Cairo – the line kept on breaking – it was to hear Constance tell her, 'There's no doubt in my mind that your leaving for Minya caused his stroke. He was very, very worried about you, he talked all the time about what a terrible thing it was for you to be sent there. Those who sent you there are responsible for his stroke, those wretched creatures.'

'How are you holding up?' Claire asked her. Constance was nearing her eighty-first birthday.

'I couldn't have managed without Batta and her daughter. They take turns. Batta is here during the day, her daughter does the night shift. Thank God for the two of them. Batta is a real gem. Just like her mother used to be, God bless her soul. I cannot say the same about the daughter, but I should not complain. No five minutes go by without him calling for someone, whether or not he needs anything.'

'Has Charlotte been helping out?'

'I cannot expect her to help much. She's busy getting ready for Germany. She has been shopping with Gabrielle. I have a feeling she's finding it a major adjustment to be living with Gabrielle. It cannot be easy. Alexandre wants to talk to you. Let me hand him the phone.'

Alexandre's voice on the phone was faint; usually it was clear and strong. He started by saying, 'Don't worry about me,' then, immediately asked, 'When are you coming. When? Soon, I hope.'

Claire promised she would do her best to come to Cairo within the next four weeks.

Two days later, in the middle of the night, Alexandre fell on his way to the bathroom – the one time he had not rung the bell for help – and fractured his hip. He underwent an operation the next day.

Gabrielle cabled the news to Claire.

It would take Claire three days to obtain permission to go to Cairo. The director of the Minya store had to refer the matter to his superior in Alexandria, who had to refer the matter to the corporate headquarters in Cairo. 'I would think that you'll stop working soon then,' the Minya director told her as he handed her written authorization for a week's emergency leave. 'Don't you think?'

Claire ignored the question.

For once sympathetic, her co-workers, even her tormentor from the appliance department, seemed sorry for her. During her three days of waiting for the authorization, her chair was not moved once, the electric fan was moved back close to her department, no remarks were made. Thanks to young Mona, everyone in the store knew about her situation.

Three nights in a row, Claire went to the Greek Club to play bridge. Staying in her hotel room was too oppressive, the question of what to do should Alexandre never walk again – a likely outcome at his age – gnawed at her.

At the club, she made the acquaintance of a middle-aged Greek woman, a paediatrician, who would become a good friend. The woman was still living in Minya because of a twenty-year-long affair with a man unwilling to leave his disabled wife, something for which his lover admired him.

During those three days of waiting, it seemed to Claire that she could perhaps get used to life in Minya as long as the atmosphere in the store remained serene.

* * *

Coming out of the train in the Ramses train station, despite the sea of people, Claire spotted Gabrielle and Charlotte before they saw her. It would have been hard to miss Gabrielle – tall and with striking salt-and-pepper hair. Of her three daughters, Charlotte was the smallest. Wide-hipped, with a crop of curly jet-black hair and an olive complexion, she was by far the most Egyptian-looking. Aunt and niece were unsmiling.

'Is it possible that I arrived too late?' Claire thought as she made her way through the crowd. The train ride had been long and exhausting: no air conditioning and a one-hour delay in Beni Suef. Cairo felt almost as hot as Minya. It was a blistering end of August all over Egypt.

When Gabrielle and Charlotte saw her, they waved and hurried in her direction.

Before the usual hug and kiss, Gabrielle said, 'It happened early this morning, he became delirious yesterday. He kept calling you and calling his mother.' After a brief pause, Gabrielle went on, her voice uncharacteristically mellow, 'He also called for Nicolas a couple of times.'

Pale despite the heat, Claire turned towards her daughter and asked, 'Were you at the hospital this morning?'

'No,' Charlotte said, quickly adding, 'but we were on our way to the hospital when it happened. Nuni was there.' Charlotte, her sisters and Gabrielle's daughter Aida called their Aunt Constance 'Nuni.'

Claire took a deep breath, looked away for a second, then asked, 'How is she taking it?'

'Better than one would have expected. She said she could not have looked after him, that she is too old for that. And, with you in Minya, there was no obvious solution,' Gabrielle answered.

'She said that?'

'More or less.'

'I see.'

'I brought the car. I'm driving. Do you want to go home first?'

'Yes, take me home first. I'll call the hospital.' To Charlotte, Claire then said, 'He loved you very much.'

Charlotte whispered, looking awkward, 'Yes, I know.'

A few minutes later, while Gabrielle was driving, shouting warnings out of her window to drivers and pedestrians alike, Claire, seated next to her, turned to the back and said, 'Charlotte, you shouldn't judge your father on the basis of the man he became late in life.

You've known him as an elderly man to whom life had dealt blows. You've known him as irascible and difficult. There was a time when he was an altogether different man.'

'What's the story behind my name?' Charlotte asked.

'What do you mean?' Claire asked.

'Nuni once told me that Father had insisted on giving me this name, and when I asked her why, she laughed and said that one of his first loves was a Charlotte. Is it true? Not that I would mind if it is. I'm just curious.'

'It's true. But it was not one of his early loves. He was already in his mid-thirties then. Charlotte was the woman he fell in love with when he spent a few months in Switzerland during his two years of travel in Europe, after he had cashed in his pension as a civil servant.'

'He told you about her?'

'Yes he did.'

'And you did not mind his wanting to name me after her?'

'No.'

'Not at all?'

'I don't think so.'

'So, what happened to that love story?'

'She was married.'

'How long after that did you meet him?'

'Five years or so.'

'How old were you the first time you met him in Uncle Yussef's office? You told me, but I'm not sure anymore whether you said sixteen or seventeen.'

'Fifteen as a matter of fact, about to turn sixteen.'

'It's really hard to believe that you were almost three years younger than me when you fell in love with him.'

'It did not happen on the spot.'

'Tell me again how it all started. It's such a great story. Tell me everything! I want to hear all the details,' Charlotte said, becoming all animated.

'I had met him a few times in Uncle Yussef's office. Uncle Yussef and Aunt Farida were all taken by him. They thought he was very clever, very witty. After that, I met him at one of Uncle Yussef's Sunday lunches. He sat next to me and talked to me about Stendhal, about *The Charterhouse of Parma*, which he considered superior to *The Red and the Black*. I disagreed. He was surprised to hear I had read both. He said that women generally preferred *The Red and the Black*. He had a very engaging conversation, a very engaging voice too.'

'And then?'

'A few days after that lunch, I was studying for the *bac*, getting ready for the philosophy test. I was certain that the notion of courage would be central to one of the essay topics so I was thinking of possible opening lines, pacing up and down the balcony which was right above Uncle Yussef's office. When I tried to get back in the apartment, someone had locked the door (Claire omitted to tell Charlotte that she had taken refuge on the balcony to avoid hearing the voices of her mother and sister who were in the midst of another of their many arguments; their voices were too distracting for her to concentrate in her bedroom, too upsetting too). Instead of knocking, I decided to step onto a ledge to get to my bedroom balcony, as my balcony door was open. Just as I was about to grip the railing, I slipped and fell on the veranda of Uncle Yussef's office, where he and your father happened to be sitting, having coffee.'

Charlotte was riveted although she already knew the story.

'When I came to, it was with your father bent over me, his hand on my brow, saying, "She'll be all right." Uncle Yussef was in such a state that your father took charge and had the *suffragis* carry me to our apartment, where they put me on my bed. In the meantime the doctor, whose clinic was directly opposite Uncle Yussef's office, was called. Apparently I slept for almost a full day after that, and when I woke up, I was told that the first word I uttered was "Alexandre." On my desk, there was a big bouquet of flowers he had sent. My mother decreed that I was in love with him.'

'Were you?'

'It's all a bit of a blur now. In any case, my mother saying so caused me to think I was.'

'So your mother was in favor, even though he was thirty-seven and you were sixteen?'

'She wanted a male presence in the family to counteract Uncle Yussef. Your father seemed like a man who could provide that counterweight. Besides, as I said, he had a lot of charm.' Claire refrained from disclosing to Charlotte that Gabrielle too had been initially enthusiastic about Alexandre.

'We're almost there,' Gabrielle announced in a gruff voice.

Still talking to her daughter, Claire said, 'His being so difficult the last couple of years is typical of people who have had strokes. The doctor said so.' Then she added, as though in passing, 'He introduced you to the world of cinema. Remember the year I was in Beirut, when he allowed you to skip school and took you to the cinema instead? You got to see a series of Russian movies, one based on a Chekhov short story, *The Lady with the Lapdog*; he wrote to me about that movie, saying how much he had enjoyed it.'

'I remember that movie. I remember liking it. We also got to see several Yussef Chahine movies. Many featured Faten Hamama.

I thought she was wonderful. Even better than Vivien Leigh in *Gone with the Wind*,' Charlotte said, warming to the subject.

'That was the year you dreamed of becoming a movie director.'

'After my degree in anthropology perhaps,' Charlotte said, 'I might do documentaries.'

'I think you should,' Claire said. 'Youthful enthusiasms can take you a long way if you cultivate them.'

'I'll drop you and park the car,' Gabrielle said, her tone still surly.

'Perhaps I should walk over to Constance's place,' Claire said as she stepped out of the car.

'She's waiting for you at home. With Batta. They have become inseparable,' Gabrielle said. 'You come with me to the garage. I might need your help.'

Charlotte looked at her mother.

'Go with your aunt,' Claire said and, with a quick gesture of the head, indicated to her daughter not to make a fuss.

* * *

Since the death of Uncle Yussef, the building in which Claire lived was becoming grubbier by the day. His son took no interest in the building whatsoever. 'Why would I and how can I, if I cannot raise the rents? I will the day they do away with rent controls,' he explained whenever the subject came up.

Time had not inured Claire to the building's degradation. She felt both shame and revulsion at her surroundings. Most buildings in downtown Cairo were suffering from neglect but none as much as hers. The glass panes of many windows in the stairwell and landings were broken. The windows overlooked an internal courtyard with a secondary staircase intended for service people. That courtyard was now littered with garbage, in which mice and cockroaches nested. Instead of the old marble fountain at the building's entrance was an ugly kiosk rented to a man who sold cold drinks and peanuts.

On entering the building that evening, Claire paid no attention to the state it was in. She was thinking of Alexandre, trying to relive the man he had been when they first met. She found herself listing characteristics, but that was the extent of it: tall, sinewy, dark-haired and fair of complexion, often wearing the tarbush, often with some clever repartees, often doing the handsome thing; well-read, and well-informed; sought after in salons, impetuous but soft-hearted; in sum, a man with plenty of charm to make up for his lack of means and obvious career trajectory after he had left the civil service, where he had held the position of permanent secretary in the law department of Egypt's prestigious Ministry of Public Works. It was the death of that man years earlier, not his death the day before, that struck Claire as the truly terrible thing, as she waited for the only working elevator in her building to reach the ground floor.

Omar, the doorman, a quarrelsome sort with whom Alexandre used to argue almost daily, paid her his condolences and, standing quietly by her side with her suitcase in hand, managed even to look affected.

Constance and Batta were sitting in the hallway when Claire let herself in. They both got up. Next to ample Batta dressed in black, Constance, also dressed in black, looked like a miniature. With a small limp due to two consecutive fractures of the same hip, she walked towards Claire. Batta followed.

Claire kissed them both. Constance's eyes misted. Crying, Batta said, 'I'll miss him. He had a short fuse but a good heart, and that's what matters. I'll never forget his wise words when my husband took another wife, "Batta, you're too good for him. He does not deserve you. He'll come to that realization sooner or later. Then he'll be knocking at your door and you may not want him back." He was right.' After dabbing her eyes, she added, 'I'll go and prepare some fresh lemonade, but first let me put your suitcase in the bedroom.'

'Did he suffer much?' Claire asked Constance.

'No ... well, perhaps a bit ... not much though, not much.'

'What happened? In the end, I mean?' Claire asked.

'Kidney failure, the doctor said. If he had not been such a heavy smoker, things might have turned out differently.'

For a moment, the two women, both still standing, were silent, each looking pensive.

Claire broke the silence. 'Thank you for all you did. It could not have been easy for you. You were very close to each other.'

Constance nodded, her eyes again misty. 'We quarreled a lot though. We always did. But I suppose that's natural; we were so close in age. He was my mother's favorite. Of the four of us, she liked him the best. She spoilt him and he humored her. After my father died, the two of them squandered the family's assets. She never, never thought about tomorrow. He let her do as she pleased. He shouldn't have. He was after all the oldest son.'

'So, she's still begrudging him that,' Claire thought.

The two women were quiet again.

'He could have been a real somebody,' Constance suddenly said. 'He had so many talents. To think that when he graduated from the Jesuit school with prizes in French literature, philosophy, history, Arabic, Latin and English too, the principal told my mother he had a brilliant future ahead of him.' Constance shook her head. 'Who would have predicted it? Who? If only he had stayed in the ministry where he was much appreciated but no, he got it into his head that the working environment was no longer congenial and quit even though they wanted him to stay on.' Constance sighed then said, 'Well, you know the story.'

'Yes,' Claire said. She knew the story, one version – Gabrielle's version – being that Alexandre had wanted to quit anyway to go roaming in Europe, which he did for a couple of years. That was when he fell in love, in Switzerland, with the woman called Charlotte, apparently a countess.

'I know that Gabrielle thinks he resigned on a whim because he'd had enough working. She's wrong. He liked his work and was much respected. Would King Fuad have awarded him a decoration, if he had not been highly regarded?' Constance asked. 'Would he?'

Claire speculated, 'Perhaps he left because he knew that, as an Italian, he would start facing difficulties in the ministry. Times were changing. Nationalist sentiments were running high. It was the Saad Zaghlul era. It was 1924 after all. Perhaps he thought that, for men like him, the writing was on the wall.' She felt dizzy all of a sudden and said, 'Let's leave the past alone, now we must organize the funeral. I ought to talk to your cousin George since he is in charge of the Conti crypt. I presume he knows about Alexandre.'

'He does. He came to the hospital twice.'

George Conti was a rich man. Unlike Alexandre, who quit studying law to work in the Ministry of Public Works, George completed his law studies but never practised. He was interested in making money. Always discreet about his wealth he would escape notice under the Nasser regime. Had Alexandre outlived him, as his one and only first male cousin he would have stood to inherit a substantial fortune. The two men were exactly the same age.

'It was really good of George to come to the hospital,' Constance said. 'As you know, he was barely on speaking terms with Alexandre. But family is family, and George is a family man.' After breathing a heavy sigh, she went on, 'His mother and ours were as different as can be. His mother was a penny-pinching Copt, who never touched a drop of liquor; ours, a spendthrift Greek, who did not mind a glass or two of wine. No wonder they never got along. We would have been infinitely better off with a mother like George's. Alexandre would have hated to hear me say that. We would have ended up in a big fight. He was blind to our mother's faults and she to his. I loved her but I loved her with open eyes.'

Claire had heard all this before. 'I expect Simone will be able to make it to the funeral, but I'm not sure Djenane will. Her theater group is touring in France. It's her first big role,' she said apologetically.

Extremely protective of Claire's three girls as she was of Gabrielle's daughter Aida, who had just got married and was living in Washington D.C., Constance leaped to Djenane's defense: 'Djenane should do what is best for her. He would understand.'

'Would he?' Claire was not so sure.

'He loved you deeply,' Constance said unexpectedly.

Claire bowed her head. For never-married Constance, love seemed such a straightforward thing: he loves her; she loves him; she does not love him; they love each other ... Constance had no difficulties seeing love, or the absence of it.

They heard the click of a key. Gabrielle and Charlotte walked in.

'Well, I'll go home now,' Constance said and got up.

'Charlotte, walk your aunt home,' Claire told her daughter.

'No need to. Batta will walk with me part of the way.' Constance hugged Charlotte.

'Good evening, Gabrielle,' she told her sister-in-law.

'I'll walk you home,' Gabrielle offered.

'No, no, Batta will.'

'As you please then.' Gabrielle was visibly annoyed by what she took to be a rebuff. 'Doesn't Batta want to go straight home though?'

Just then Batta appeared in the room, shrouded in her *melayah*, insisting that she would walk '*Mazmazel* Constance' home.

Gabrielle stormed off to the kitchen.

Claire walked them to the door, saying to Constance, 'I don't need to tell you that you're as welcome here as you have always been. You have the key.'

'I know, I know,' Constance said, looking all of a sudden grief-stricken though she did not give way to tears. Batta put her arm around her. 'I have some things for you,' Constance continued. 'They're in an envelope. Alexandre's keepsakes. When he moved in with me a few weeks ago, he brought the envelope along. I'll bring it tomorrow. I meant to today, but it slipped my mind.'

Just before starting down the stairs – like Alexandre, she avoided elevators – Constance turned around to tell Claire, 'I was the oldest of the four and yet I'm still here, and they're gone. That's not right.'

The first time Claire met her, Constance had been standing next to her sister Helene and their mother on the landing of their apartment on Ramses Street not far from the train station: from their balcony, the three women had seen Claire and Alexandre enter the building and were waiting on the landing to greet the couple whose marriage was to take place only two days later. Constance was in her early forties, Helene in her mid-thirties, and their mother in her sixties. Wearing somber clothes, their hair pulled in severe buns, without any make-up except for some kohl, they had seemed ancient to eighteen-year-old Claire, the daughters barely distinguishable from the mother. At first, Claire had not known what to talk about – neither to the mother nor to the sisters. They had given her the impression of living such a cloistered life. There were no books in sight in the apartment, which had surprised her as Alexandre was a big reader. Constance and Helene had gone to her school, La Mère de Dieu. This would give her a subject of conversation but barely. Half-way through the visit, on discovering that Constance loved to draw and finding her sketches really quite good, Claire, who also drew well, had warmed to Alexandre's older sister. Yet, when the visit was over, she had asked herself whether she was doing the right thing to be marrying into a family so different from hers, and also whether Alexandre had so delayed introducing her to his family for fear she might get cold feet.

Standing by the entrance door of her apartment, as Constance had on that first meeting, Claire wondered what had become of Constance's drawings, then heard Gabrielle, in the background, telling Charlotte that dinner was on the table.

* * *

Bread, cheese and watermelon were laid out on the dining-room table.

'You must be hungry,' Gabrielle told Claire.

'Not really,' Claire said, 'but thank you all the same.'

'Not feeling well?' Gabrielle asked. 'You look pale. Charlotte, get your mother a glass of water.'

'I think I'm getting a migraine.'

'Eat something then. It may ward it off.'

Claire would have preferred to go and lie down in her room, yet, out of politeness, felt obliged to take a bite.

'When are you thinking of holding the funeral?' Gabrielle asked.

'It will depend on when Simone gets back. We should be hearing within the next twenty-four hours.'

'How long can you stay?'

'They authorized a one-week leave but I would think that, in the circumstances, it can be extended, though I would not count on it. They want me out. That's clear. They'll do all they can to drive me into the wall and corner me into resigning.'

'You must go and see your lawyer first thing in the morning.'

'First thing in the morning, I'll go to the hospital, though it's true that he goes to his office so early that I may be able to catch him on my way. Where's Charlotte?'

'On the phone probably. By the way, I bumped into Marie Sussa on Kasr al-Nil Street yesterday. She just returned from Beirut. There's apparently turmoil brewing in the Palestinian camps. People are saying that this was bound to happen; that Lebanon would become an indirect casualty of the Six-Day War.'

'So you're suggesting that I'm better off in Minya than I would have been in Beirut,' Claire said. Gabrielle had been against her moving to Beirut.

'I am merely telling you what Marie said, namely, that there are problems on the horizon in Lebanon. There's instability in the air.'

'I think I ought to lie down', Claire said. 'I cannot afford getting a migraine now.'

'Would you like me to come along to the hospital?' Gabrielle asked.

Knowing how much her sister dreaded hospitals since Nicolas's death, Claire declined. 'Can you send a telegram to Iris though? She was fond of Alexandre. So was Anastase. Bella happens to be in Geneva right now so she'll find out from them. As for Aristote, I am certain that Constance will contact him.' Claire fell silent, recalling how Bella and Aristote had met through Alexandre, and Anastase and Iris through Aristote. The love matches – she and Alexandre, Bella and Aristote – had failed, whereas the marriage of reason – Iris and Anastase – had succeeded.

* * *

Rather than to her room, Claire went to Alexandre's at the far end of the apartment. She sat on the narrow single bed next to which hung his mother's old cross. Not much of a churchgoer, he was nevertheless quite attached to the cross. The room was badly in need of refurbishing, the paint uneven, the hardwood floor peeling, and the few pieces of furniture were ill-assorted. Claire had offered, several times, to refurbish the room but each time he had refused, saying it was not worth it, not worth her assuming any extra financial responsibilities. Over the years, he would refuse to come out of his room the few evenings a year she gave dinner or bridge parties. 'How can I show my face at your gatherings? Put yourself in my shoes,' he screamed once, after she had suggested he might at least put in a brief appearance. Entitled to a substantial pension on leaving the ministry, he had cashed in the biggest chunk he could and spent that handsome sum on travel and high living in Europe in his mid-thirties. For several years after he came back, he worked – mostly for Yussef Sahli – and what he earned, he spent. Once he stopped working, without a penny other than the derisory amount left in the pension, joining gatherings attended by men of means – some courting his wife – was too painful a reminder of his social fall.

'You put yourself in mine,' she had retorted. 'Am I supposed to relinquish all of my social life?' She had gone on throwing parties – not as often as she would have liked – during which he would stay in this bleak room.

He was in his early sixties when he quit working for Yussef Sahli and no other job came his way except for the occasional translation. From then on, his morning routine would consist of waking up at five o'clock, showering – always with cold water even during the coldest months of the year – preparing breakfast for the girls, paying a quick visit to Constance if they had not had an altercation the previous evening, then going to the Café Riche where he read the French and Arabic papers, and met men his age or older. They were all retired. The men in his group, Muslims and Copts, included an Azhar scholar and a couple of ex-diplomats who, like him, had fallen upon hard times. The only *Khawaga* in the group, he fit right in thanks to his impeccable Arabic, tarbush, and years of public service. At lunch, he would return home, spend the early afternoon buried in his dictionaries or some biography. The evenings he would spend at Groppi's with the same set. They would talk about the past and international affairs, avoiding the dangerous subject of domestic politics. Now and then though, they slipped and discussed contemporary events in Egypt, after which they would joke, with some nervousness, that their age should shield them from trouble. Alexandre had not been particularly opposed to Nasser but then why should he have been, having nothing to lose? After Groppi's, he would stop by the grocery store to buy cheese and olives, by the bakery to get some fresh bread, then, from a street vendor standing by the bakery, he often bought a lottery ticket before returning home for dinner. He would be in bed by nine o'clock or 9.30 at the latest – just as Claire was getting ready to go out. That had been the rhythm of his life during its last fifteen years.

In its austerity, its down-and-out quality, his room resembled Claire's hotel room in Minya. 'Enough,' she thought, 'Enough!' and got up brusquely, which was unusual for her. Instead of going to lie down as she had intended all along, she grabbed her handbag in the dining room and told Gabrielle and Charlotte that she was going to Constance's place and would be back in half an hour.

'But why?' Gabrielle asked.

'She has something to give me.'

'What about your headache? Why not send Charlotte?'

'No, no, I'll be back quickly. I need some fresh air.'

'That's not like you.' Gabrielle said. 'You usually prefer to be indoors.'

'If Simone calls, make sure one of you takes the details of her flight,' Claire said, rushing out of the room.

* * *

Claire would open the big brown envelope in which Alexandre had kept his mementoes the next morning, at daybreak.

First, she took out of the envelope a large picture she had never seen before. It was of the opening of the Egyptian parliament with bulky, sullen-looking King Fuad on his raised throne in the middle; below him, standing, Saad Zaghlul was giving a speech, flanked on each side by the seated parliamentarians. Also seated but around a table, at the center, were the various ministries' permanent civil servants. Amongst them was Alexandre, easily recognizable by virtue of his extremely erect posture, the sharpness of his jawbone and the fairness of his complexion.

Next, she took out of the envelope a small box containing the royal decree awarding Alexandre his decoration. She took out the medal too.

Then she examined a picture of her taken at the zoo shortly after her memorable fall from the fourth floor. Just sixteen years old, she had recently had her hair cut in a slightly boyish bob.

Encircled by an old elastic band were three pictures of three women in their twenties or early thirties. One very pretty, one less so, and one with a penetrating gaze under heavy eyebrows. No names were written on the back of the pictures, only the place and the year in which they were taken: Cairo 1922, Geneva 1925, and Zurich 1926. The one taken in Cairo – the picture of the very pretty young woman – would have been, Claire guessed, a picture of a woman from a wealthy background, to whom Alexandre had been quasi-engaged. As told by Constance, the story was that he had broken up with the pretty young woman after hearing of rumors that he was after her money. His explanation had been simpler: 'It was not meant to be,' he told Claire the only time she asked him about it.

Written in pencil – Alexandre wrote mostly in pencil – and folded many times over was the draft of a letter he had sent Claire ten years earlier, in which he was saying that, though degraded in his own eyes to find himself in that equivocal position, he could not but accept the liaison she was having at the time because it brought her material comforts he could not provide; he was referring to a car and a driver. Claire remembered the letter all too well. To read the draft – not much different from the letter she had received – upset her more than it ought to since she was already familiar with its contents. Pity, but also anger for letting herself again be moved to pity, welled up in her: if only she could have been left with traces of Alexandre's former self as opposed to being confronted afresh with the diminished man! Tempted for a second to discard the draft letter, she nonetheless refolded it as neatly as she had found it and put it back in the envelope. To throw it away seemed to her a disrespectful and callous thing to do.

From the envelope, she pulled one more piece of paper – a tiny scrap that would have come out of the small notebooks Alexandre typically carried in his shirt or coat pocket, on which he would jot down thoughts, summarize articles, and keep track of sources he might want to consult some day. Occasionally, he would copy a few lines of a passage in a book or poem that had struck his fancy. The hand holding the piece of paper was firm but the corner of Claire's mouth trembled as she read the few lines of a poem that Alexandre had copied:

> *How difficult for one who has failed,*
> *for one who has declined, to learn the new*
> *language of poverty and new ways*
> *...........................*
>
> *How will he face the cold glances that will*
> *indicate to him that he is a burden!*

Claire stuck that piece of paper back into the envelope, then reached for a big bag Constance had given her. It contained the frock-coat Alexandre had worn on meeting King Fuad at Ras al-Tin Palace in Alexandria to receive his award. The coat was as new, though it reeked of naphthalene. Claire decided that the coat would go to Simone, the medal to Djenane, and the accompanying decree to

Charlotte. Her hope was that this small legacy would restore the man in their eyes.

* * *

Even though he had converted to Roman Catholicism at the age of sixteen, since he was to be buried in the Conti family crypt in the Greek Orthodox cemetery of old Cairo, Claire thought it best to hold Alexandre's funeral in a Greek Orthodox church. She had not forgotten the fuss made by the priests in charge of the cemetery over her little boy's burial.

During the service, which she could not follow as it was in Greek, Claire wondered whether the priest officiating was saying something about Alexandre and if so, what? Alexandre's profile was singular even in the context of the hybrid milieu to which he belonged: an Italian who wore the tarbush; spoke, read and wrote Arabic like an Egyptian; went to a French school; Greek Orthodox by birth; may or may not have been of Greek origin on his father's side, but certainly was on his mother's; a convert to Roman Catholicism yet buried in a Greek Orthodox cemetery; a man who declared he had a profound Christian faith but would never spend more than five minutes in a church because they made him claustrophobic and subject to dizzy spells during mass, so he said; a man with a privileged childhood and rich and powerful friends yet penniless at the end of his life ... to say nothing of his marriage so little like a marriage.

Had she ever loved him?

Yussef Sahli's wife Farida attended the funeral with Aristote, Bella's estranged husband. Her mind not altogether there, she asked the young man standing next to her twice during the ceremony, 'Who are you?' and also asked him, 'Remind me, who is it we're burying?' The young man was Hamid Hassanein, Claire's lawyer. His father, Alexandre's friend Maher, was in bed with pneumonia.

The evening of the funeral, Iris telephoned Claire from Geneva. 'I was very fond of Alexandre,' she began, 'my father talked to me a lot about him towards the end of his life. He said more than once that Alexandre had too much pride and that was his problem. He said he was a man who had not adjusted to the changing times; that he belonged to a bygone era. It was clear that, in spite of their quarrel, he was still fond of him. I got the feeling he would have liked to see Alexandre one last time.'

'It's all so unfortunate,' was all that Claire said in response, suspecting Iris to have made up this story. She did not tell Iris that, in her uncle's dying days, she had suggested to Alexandre he go see him. His response came back to her almost word for word:

'What would be the point? To pretend I am no longer angry with him for treating me like his flunkey all the years I worked for him? Summoning me to his office up to thirty times an hour – yes, up to thirty times – to tell me drivel! Calling me at home at dawn or at midnight to say something he could have easily told me in his office! Using me as entertainer – please don't interrupt me – yes, entertainer at his soirées! When he was in need of someone to animate the conversation, he would not rest until I agreed to go, which I usually did for your sake. But that one evening he insisted I go to his place to play a game of backgammon with a potential business partner, I had had it. You know the rest! No Claire, I won't go see him. I don't wish him ill, but I cannot pretend all is forgotten.'

Had Alexandre ever wondered about the nature of her uncle's affection for her? That was a subject neither he nor she had ever raised.

After Iris's phone call came a telegram from Bella, '*I expect it will be hard for you ... in a certain way. Love, Bella.*'

Bella had guessed right: it proved to be hard on Claire, in a certain way. Alexandre's death should have brought her relief – if only from the scenes he customarily made – scenes with Constance and Gabrielle, both as irascible as he was, but also with the girls, with the household help, with herself. He and her uncle had been alike in that respect, except that Alexandre's explosiveness was more understandable; there were good reasons for it. So yes, his death ought to have made life easier for her. And it did, though without bringing her any light-heartedness. Instead, after Alexandre's death, Claire's spirits sagged. When she returned to Minya, her co-workers treated her with the courtesy accorded the newly widowed, but that did not last long. Within a few weeks, the harassment resumed, with management doing nothing about it. It was now clear to all in the store that she was not about to quit. Her workdays required a staying power she managed to summon, but, perhaps precisely because they were so grueling, she found herself running over in her mind, many times a day, what her life might have been without Alexandre. The more she let her mind wander, the more she held it against herself that she stayed in her marriage – albeit only with one foot – for her staying did not seem to have made anyone happier; neither him, nor her, nor her daughters, who had had to live in an atmosphere of perpetual tension. In Minya, Claire's character took a morose turn. To combat that tendency – her mother's specter loomed over her – she became an assiduous member of the bridge group at the Greek Club.

At the end of her two years in Minya, she concluded that the time she had spent there had not been all that bad. She had made some friends, kept her bridge skills going, read the *Forsyte Saga* in

English as well as much of Edith Wharton's work, and discovered Natalie Sarraute. And she had got to know Hamid Hassanein, whose selflessness, humility and dedication in fighting the battles of the little guys harked back to her youthful spirit and made her think of her father. Thanks to her lawyer, in the bittersweet make-up of Claire's character, some sweetness remained. When she returned to Cairo, he urged her not to bear too much of a grudge against her co-workers as their reaction was understandable. She assured him she had understood (which she had), but it did not made the experience any easier.

Claire had been back in Cairo for a couple of months when, following a meeting aimed at bringing about a reconciliation between the PLO and King Hussein of Jordan, Nasser died after collapsing with severe chest pains. He had already begun steering the country to the right – a move now accelerated by his successor, Sadat. For Claire's lawyer and his leftist comrades, who had seemed to be gaining momentum after the June 1967 war, the future looked bleak again. Their days of being hounded were not over. And soon, the Muslim Brotherhood would overtake the communists in popularity, making Claire remark that Nasser may have been an aberration.

1978: Constance

Charlotte was back in Cairo. Perhaps to stay, she announced on arrival. Filming her documentary on Egyptian women would give her some sense of what life in Egypt had become and therefore some basis on which to make up her mind. She had been living in Montreal where she had just completed a Ph.D. in anthropology while studying filmmaking on the side. Briefly married, she was at present unattached, had no children and wanted none. 'You may change your mind,' Claire told her. 'You're only twenty-seven.'

It had been ten years since her father died; eight since Sadat became Egypt's president; four since he embarked on his program of economic liberalization; two since he dissolved the Arab socialist party; one since his trip to Jerusalem and speech at the Knesset; and barely four months since the death of Constance at the age of ninety-one. Constance had died in an old people's home founded seventy-five years earlier thanks to a donation made by a Conti, one of Constance's uncles. The home, on the outskirts of Cairo, took her in free of charge, more because she was poor than because of the donation.

Charlotte's toying with the idea of returning to Cairo delighted her Aunt Gabrielle, a firm believer in Egypt's future. Though it would of course benefit her to have one of her daughters in Cairo, Claire had mixed feelings as she was less optimistic about Egypt's future. The resurgence of the Muslim Brotherhood – women in the streets of Cairo were beginning to wear the *higab* – coupled with the weakening of the secular left concerned her. She was not sure that Sadat's brand of political liberalization would go much further. Her lawyer, whom she still saw on occasion, thought not and predicted that stifling political life would exacerbate fundamentalist feelings.

'If you're really serious about trying to make a life here, you ought to look into getting Egyptian citizenship,' she told Charlotte that morning over breakfast. 'Unfortunately, neither my being Egyptian nor your being born here entitles you to it, so I wouldn't be too hopeful, but who knows … there may be a way.'

'Can't your lawyer do something about it?' Gabrielle asked. Now living in the same building as Claire, she had stopped by for breakfast. Whenever Gabrielle referred to Claire's lawyer, her intonation acquired a certain edge. His politics still rubbed her the wrong way.

'I'll arrange for Charlotte to see him. I'm sure he'll do his best but he cannot make miracles.'

'What made you decide to give Egypt a try?' Gabrielle asked Charlotte. 'You seemed happy in Montreal.'

'I am. It's not a question of my not being happy there,' Charlotte said. 'However, for some reason I cannot even explain to myself, I feel that spending part of my adult life in Egypt is important, that I left too early. I feel a bit like I deserted the country.'

'I can tell you one thing,' Gabrielle said, 'you look Egyptian. Your years abroad did not change that. You lost weight but all the girls in Egypt have too, no matter their social class.'

Charlotte laughed. 'So I fit right in,' she said. She was about to add that her desire to come back to live in Cairo had surfaced soon after Constance's death but stopped herself, mindful of the old tensions between her two aunts. Was this a coincidence, or could the death of an aunt to whom she had been strongly attached as a child trigger this longing for a homeland she had left quite young?

'Well, I must leave you now or else I'll be late for work,' Gabrielle said. Though nearing seventy, Gabrielle was in charge of an haute couture house – a job offered to her a year after she retired as a supervisor in state-run schools. She loved her job, as well as pointing out that she owed it to Sadat's liberalizing policies; under Nasser, there would have been no such job for her. Claire too was working four days a week in a friend's bookstore.

Now much fonder of her Aunt Gabrielle than she had been as a child, Charlotte walked her to the door. 'It's a good time to talk to Mother about Nuni,' Charlotte thought on her way back to the dining room.

* * *

The evening before leaving Montreal, Charlotte had sat at her desk and, on the spur of the moment, begun writing a piece on her Aunt Nuni. She had continued writing on the plane as well as during her brief stay in London, where her sister Simone lived. In Cairo she had written more and had just finished the piece which she intended to show to her mother. But, before doing that, she wanted to hear her mother's perspective on her aunt's life.

'By the way,' Charlotte began as she poured herself another cup of tea, 'how did Gabrielle and Nuni get along during the last years of her life?'

'They made their peace,' Claire said. 'Gabrielle was quite good about visiting her in the home. She saw her once a week. Sometimes Batta went along.'

'You went too, I presume?'

'Not as often.'

'How come?' Charlotte asked, surprised.

Claire frowned. 'I found it hard.'

'I would have thought that Gabrielle would find it harder.'

'It's hospitals that Gabrielle has an aversion to.'

'And yours is to old people's homes?'

'To some extent, yes. But ...'

'But?'

'I found it hard to visit Constance.'

'But why? You two got along. She was extremely fond of you.'

'I know,' Claire said. 'And I admired her resilience. I thought her immensely courageous. Immensely selfless. But to be honest, I felt I had done my share and could do no more.'

Before Charlotte could say anything, Claire went on, 'Yes, yes, it was unfair of me. I should have risen above my feelings. But whenever I would visit her, I would end up reviewing my life, the choices I made or did not make, and I would end up feeling bitter. The visits dragged me down. Perhaps I identified with her.'

'How so?' Charlotte said bemused. 'I don't understand.'

'Like me, she must have had many regrets.'

'I think you're projecting,' Charlotte said heatedly.

'Look, she ended up destitute and alone, in an old people's home, in a kind of dormitory. How could she not have had regrets?'

Avoiding the question, Charlotte said almost reluctantly, 'I wrote something about her.'

'About Constance?' Claire asked.

'Yes. Why? Do you find that strange?'

'I didn't know you wrote. That's all.'

'I don't write. I just wrote this one little piece. If you feel like reading it, you can have a look at it but only if you want to.'

'I'll read it,' Claire said without much enthusiasm. She found the subject of Constance's life painful, both because she deemed it a very sad life and because it somehow brought home her own failings and failures.

After reading the piece, she told Charlotte, 'At your age I might have written something similar.' Would she have though?

* * *

I did not do right by Nuni during the last years of her life, which she spent in an old people's home on the outskirts of Cairo. I should have sent her letters or at least postcards yet seldom did. I was too wrapped up in a life so distant from the life in which she played such a big part – my life as a child and adolescent growing up in Egypt – to feel remorse for my neglect. News of her death left me feeling awkward – the kind of awkwardness that covers up a bad conscience.

Whenever I am in Cairo, I walk past the building where she lived. Her apartment, on the ground floor, has been converted into a travel agency. She got a bit of money for it when she gave it up, only very little though. The man who took it over had had designs on it for years before she finally agreed to move out. She had no one to back her in her dealings with him except for her cousin George and he was eager for her to move into the home as quickly as possible. It would free him from feeling responsible for her well-being. She had no income other than the rents two boarders paid her, and a tiny monthly sum bequeathed to her by a brother of his, to whom she had been engaged in her youth. So when the man who wanted to turn her apartment into a travel agency renewed his offer, George Conti encouraged her to take the money and move. Both he and Nuni were well into their eighties by then.

I can imagine Nuni in the evenings, sitting by her window, the shutters half-open, watching the comings and goings in her lane, her cheek firmly pressed against her hand, very still. When I was a child, I sat by that window too, with her by my side. During my teenage years, if I happened to be walking in her lane at five or six o'clock in the evening and did not have time to drop in, I would talk to her from underneath the window. As I think back on those days, it occurs to me that I failed Nuni long before I left Egypt, for there were times when I avoided her lane if I was in a rush, or not in the mood to talk. It was mean of me to deny her this little pleasure; she had given me so many pleasures all through my childhood. Sometimes, I even walked down the lane very fast on the sidewalk opposite her window, accelerating my pace in the hope she would not see me. If she noticed, she never complained, never once said: 'How easily you forgot the sweets I gave you behind your mother's back, the family tales I filled your child's head with, the visits to my old friends you seemed so keen on, my hand stroking your hair whenever you put your head down on my lap. Now, you run past my window without bothering to say even hello!' She never uttered a single reproach.

A life of self-abnegation and unswerving loyalty to family: people used to say that she was mad to give as much as she did and not look after herself. Even my mother, the beneficiary of much of that selflessness, used to say so.

At the end of her long life, did Nuni have any regrets? Most people would say she ought to have had many regrets. She ought to have wept a lot, wishing she could re-live her life all over again but altogether differently this time. It seems to me though that Nuni would have been unable to imagine doing it any differently than she did. Maybe she cursed the fate that befell her and forced upon her the life it did, but regrets in the sense of thinking 'If only I had done this as opposed to that', I doubt she had. I doubt she ever came to view the conduct of her life as a matter of choice. I believe that she was too old-fashioned for that sort of thinking, too tied to a notion of family solidarity which few of us today can really understand – let alone embrace. But then I may be wrong. At the end of her life, she may have come to question everything she held dear. Not having been by her side, I have no idea what thoughts crossed her mind as the end drew nearer.

My father was sixty-two years old when I was born and Nuni was in her mid-sixties. By the time I got to spend time with her, she limped on account of two fractures in her fifties. Young girls are generally acute observers of what adults wear. Through my child's eyes, Nuni always looked the same because she wore, day after day, if not quite the same outfit, very similar outfits – even on festive occasions. The seasons changed yet her outfits hardly changed. A dark blue or black skirt that covered her calf, a white or beige blouse always with sleeves, short sleeves in the summertime, long in the wintertime. On cold days, she would wear a woolen cardigan, often blue or black but sometimes gray and occasionally beige. She rarely wore a coat. She

ANNE-MARIE DROSSO

seemed to suffer neither from the heat nor from the cold. Small
and light, she did not look particularly fragile. Her gray hair
was tied in a bun set low on her nape. She wore no make-up
but for a hint of kohl powder outlining her lower eyelid. And
no jewelry except for inconspicuous brooches – so inconspicuous that they hardly counted as jewelry in my child's eyes. She
usually dabbed some light, lemony cologne behind her ears; I
could smell it when we kissed. The scent suited her. Even without the cologne, she smelled nice: fresh and clean. Her features
were angular, her lips thin and finely chiseled, her complexion
was milky, her forehead large. Though she gave the impression
of being the sort of woman who spent little time in front of the
mirror, her appearance was always tidy – from her spotless and
well-ironed blouses to her soft hair gathered in a neat bun.

I saw a picture of Nuni taken when she was sixteen years old,
in the garden of the villa where she grew up. I myself was sixteen
when my mother showed me the picture. I remember exclaim-
ing: 'It cannot be Nuni; it cannot be! If it is, will I too change
as much?' The only recognizable thing about her was her small
build. The very young woman in the picture looked graceful
and had the slimmest of waists – the size of waist that Scarlett
O'Hara struggled to preserve. Her dress was charming – white,
with an intricate lacy pattern on its bodice and a stand-up
collar that might have looked too severe on an older woman, but
in her case accentuated her youth. Her hair was full, gathered
at the top of her head with little curls framing her large forehead. While her features in the picture were a bit fuzzy, I could
tell that their overall effect was attractive. What stood out was
the feminine and self-assured way in which she carried herself.
Both the pose and the dress bespoke a young woman entering a

more mature phase of her life on an extremely favorable footing. I saw other pictures of her when she was a bit younger, also in the garden of the family villa, in the company of another girl, a neighbor who would marry King Fuad and become queen of Egypt.

Large families often have a Nuni – the unmarried aunt who lives her life vicariously through the lives of married brothers and sisters. Always present but in the background, necessary to the family's functioning but resented for that very reason, these maiden aunts usually end up in that role because they are at a disadvantage in life right from the outset: they are unattractive; or without money; or a bit slow; or fragile health-wise. But Nuni was none of these. There was money in the family, at least until her father died, and a little while after that too. It would have taken some time before her mother, together with my father, squandered the family fortune, as the legend has it. Her looks would not have been the problem – quite the contrary, as I found out from the pictures I saw. She graduated from one of Cairo's most exclusive girls' schools and won several prizes upon graduation. Outgoing and uncomplicated, she was remarkably good at languages, had a knack for drawing and was perceptive about people. Judging by her character in her sixties and seventies, she had a cheerful disposition. At the outset, a good-looking girl with quite a lot going for her. At the end, an old woman, impoverished and alone. And, in between, steady social decline resulting in an increasingly narrow life lived through a confining web of close-knit family relationships.

She was born in 1887; she died in 1978. The oldest of four children

– two girls and two boys – there was Nuni, then my father, who was close in age to her, then a girl called Helene who was five or six years' younger and died in her thirties, and last Nicolas, about ten years' younger. She survived them all, looking after each one of them, in some way or other, at different times in her life. She herself was endowed with a very strong constitution. I never heard her complain about her health, never heard her mention a headache, a stomachache or a sore throat. I never saw her take pills. Her bones were brittle; she did of course see doctors when she sustained fractures, but only then. Despite her fractures and the cane she began using in her sixties, she walked long distances, climbed stairs without ever sounding out of breath, carried grocery bags as well as heavy serving trays all the way from the bakery's oven to our place. She would serve herself only the smallest of portions of the oven-baked potato dish, the pasta with béchamel sauce, or the rice pudding and chocolate mousse she had prepared for us. What she liked best was fresh bread with a slice of cheese or a tiny bit of hallawa.

Of her father, she always spoke reverently, describing him as handsome, thoughtful and kind, and saying that his premature death at the age of fifty had been disastrous for the family. I have no idea what he did for a living. He might have been a landlord. There was money on his side of the family and he had married a girl with money, the only daughter of a Greek land-owner of Upper Egypt.

She did not speak as kindly of her mother, whom she described as spendthrift, selfish and irresponsible in the conduct of the family's affairs. She had obviously resented her mother's special closeness to the first-born son, my father. Maybe her mother had been self-ish and unwise and even irresponsible. I will never forget a scene *between Nuni and my father concerning her. Whenever they talked about very personal family matters, Nuni and my father spoke to each other in Greek or in Arabic. It was not just because they did not wish other family members (such as my mother) to understand, although that must have been a factor. They would speak in these two languages to talk about personal matters when they were alone too. The reason was, I think, that they were the languages they had spoken with their mother; the languages that sprung from deeply felt emotions. French was the language of their schooling; the language for social conversations.*

Like many of the family scenes I witnessed or overheard in my childhood, the scene concerning my grandmother took place at home in the dining room. It had begun with Nuni saying to my father in Arabic that their mother, long since dead, used to enjoy drinking a glass or two of wine. The tone of the remark was not overly critical but faintly suggested that their mother had had her weaknesses. In no time, my father and Nuni were raising their voices – he accusing her of maligning her and tarnishing her memory, she retorting that she was calling a spade a spade, as opposed to burying her head in the sand and pretending that their mother had been a saint. In the end, my father demanded that Nuni withdraw her scurrilous statements. She refused, repeating what she had said with even more vigor. So he gave her an ultimatum to withdraw the statements or to leave the house immediately. Nuni got up and left, as I expected she would.

Even when, after a particularly big quarrel with him, she stayed away, she would still send us sundry dishes and goodies for lunch. As usual, she carried them to our building but, instead of bringing them herself, she would have the bawab *carry them* up. If my mother was at home when the bawab showed up at the door, she would tell me to run down, catch up with Nuni and insist that she come up. But Nuni always refused, saying, 'I swore I would not set foot again in his home.' And I would reply, as my mother had instructed me to, 'But it's not just his home; it's ours too and we want you to come up.' Nuni would give me a big hug and say, 'One day maybe; but not today.' At home, my father would ask me how she was doing with an air of distant concern. Then he would pay her a visit; the next day she would return, telling my mother, 'It's for your sake that I came back, yours and the children's.' And so normal life would resume, until the next time.

Of Helene, her much loved sister who died in her thirties, Nuni had only good things to say, extolling her beauty, her voice (she sang like a Diva, Nuni claimed) and her fundamentally good character which, to me, suggested that Helene had not been so easy. Helene died years before I was born so I only saw her in pictures. She looked very unlike Nuni: a full body and a broad face; a big mouth and an air of languor in her gaze, which could strike some as sensual and others as artificial. Helene, too, never married. She was the ostensible cause of the break-up of Nuni's engagement to their cousin Joseph, George Conti's brother. What Nuni related to me about this chapter in the family's history is as follows: the husband of one of Joseph's many sisters took a fancy to Helene, then in her early thirties, and started dropping by their place almost every day. Apparently Helene was not inter-ested in the least in the gentleman. Besides being married to her cousin, he was short and ugly. Still, rules of hospitality required them to welcome him whenever he knocked on their door for, *after all, he was their cousin by marriage. His wife got wind of the visits and took umbrage. Her brothers, including Joseph, began casting aspersions on Helene's character. Nuni defended her, insisting she was blameless. Yet the two sisters continued to entertain the gentleman and, once, they even had to hide him behind a wardrobe when my father unexpectedly dropped in on them; they feared that my father would have made a scene, had he found out that he was still paying them visits. The criticisms grew. Nuni did not waver in her defense of Helene's reputation, and her engagement to Joseph broke up as the matter developed into a real rift between the two branches of the family.*

'But Nuni, why did you continue to entertain this man?' I asked her every time I heard the story, which I often asked her to recount. I always got the same answer: namely, that he was a most insistent sort who told them that all he wanted was a sympathetic ear. Besides, what could they do to keep him out of their home? And there was nothing going on between him and Helene anyway. On one occasion I persisted, 'But Nuni, your engagement was at stake.' She raised her eyebrows and said, 'Helene mattered more to me than Joseph.' 'But you loved him, didn't you?' I probed. And she answered, 'Not as much as you think,' to which I replied, 'But if this man did not matter to Helene, I don't see why you let him come between you and Joseph.' 'Well, I did,' she said, signaling that she would not divulge more than she had. Perhaps there was nothing more to divulge.

The gentleman's assiduous visits to their home came to an abrupt end when Helene began to feel unwell. Her heart was causing her troubles. The doctors diagnosed a fatal condition. The whole family rallied, including the Joseph branch. Years after the event, various family members still talked about how

Nuni had looked after Helene night and day, hoping against hope that her condition would improve. It did not. At the end of a long year during which poor Helene suffered a lot, she died, with Nuni by her bedside. And soon after her death, their mother became ill and Nuni looked after her for a few months, and then the mother died too.

To Nicolas, the younger brother, Nuni gave an inheritance that an uncle had left her as a small dowry for the day she would get married. This is the same uncle who had left much of his money to Cairo's Italian community. When Nuni gave the money to Nicolas, he had a good job but wanted to start a business on the side. Since he loved cars and had a mechanical aptitude, he thought of opening a garage and Nuni was more than happy to help. He was her 'adored little brother.' This is how she referred to him years after his death, never expressing regrets about the money she lost in the failed business venture. The rare times she mentioned to me the loss of that money, it was in a matter-of-fact way, without attaching blame to Nicolas. She blamed the Frenchman Nicolas had hired to run the business. She used to talk to me a lot about Nicolas's death. Helene's death she came to terms with, viewing it as an incomprehensible act of God that she had to accept. Nicolas's death was another matter. She seemed to think that, with proper care, he would have survived. Basically, she blamed Gabrielle for not doing the right thing, for not feeding him the right food, for not taking his complaints about his health seriously, for forcing him to lead an active social life when what he needed was rest. She made no bones about the fact that, after he died, she could barely look at Gabrielle. In her grief, Nuni turned a deaf ear to the doctors' hints that the operation had revealed much worse than ulcers. While they never uttered the word – almost unspeakable at the time – they tried to tell the family that Nicolas had died of cancer. Nuni, however, continued to believe, steadfastly, that he was not meant to die.

Right from the beginning of Nicolas's marriage to Gabrielle, there had been little affection between the two women. Forceful and possessive, Gabrielle resented the slightest interference in her husband's life. She wanted him wholly hers. I suppose that my mother, endowed with a conciliatory character, had been so accommodating that Nuni found it all the harder to adjust to Gabrielle's style. I gather that, caught between Nuni and his wife, Nicolas sided more often with his wife than with his sister, though he apparently always made sure not to alienate her. She never acquired, in his household, the influence – probably 'role' is a better word – she had come to acquire in ours.

There are those who probably saw Nuni as a self-important meddler. I, on the other hand, think that she simply could not conceive of watching from the sidelines whenever her brothers needed help; she could not dissociate their interests from hers, out of a profound and unshakeable sense of family solidarity. It would be unfair to conclude that her involvement and interest in their lives stemmed from the relative emptiness of hers; that she latched on to theirs because she had no life herself. From her perspective, it was in the natural order of things for her to do all she did.

After Nicolas's death Gabrielle refused to let Nuni or my father see Aida. Nuni did not yield. By enlisting the help of a mutual and understanding friend of theirs, she would secretly see my cousin. Then, one day, Gabrielle appeared at her door with an olive branch: would she mind looking after Aida the days she, Gabrielle, had to work long hours? Overjoyed, Nuni agreed. My cousin ended up spending many hours, even some nights, at Nuni's place. As far as I know, these were very happy times for both. Tensions between Gabrielle and Nuni subsided but did not entirely go away, with each saying unflattering things about the other behind her back. Still, they found a way to interact that benefited my cousin and permitted Nuni to lend a helping hand; she even took to preparing desserts for Gabrielle's receptions.

Also to their credit was their behavior about Nicolas's failed business venture. After his death, Nuni made no claim on his assets, deeming that Gabrielle, with a little girl to look after, should keep everything. Gabrielle, however, insisted on giving her some compensation in the form of modest monthly payments over a period of years. In the end then, the two women behaved – if not entirely well – at least in a civil manner towards one another.

Nuni and my father, the two siblings who lived the longest, who were closest in age, who looked alike even though he was tall and she was short, fought a lot and yet seemed indispensable to one another. She never told me she loved him, yet often told me how much he loved all of us. When she felt good about him, she cited the many prizes he had won in high school; mentioned his successful, albeit short, career as a civil servant; recalled how King Fuad had acknowledged his valuable services; alluded to his love stories with attractive women; and pointed to his generous disposition. When she was upset with him, she bemoaned the fact that Nicolas had been the youngest; declared that my father had not been up to the task of keeping the family affairs on a sound footing; decried his impulsive nature; blamed their mother for spoiling him; and portrayed my mother as an angel for putting up with him. I am not sure what she thought of him deep down, but she certainly stood by him throughout his life.

My father, who got married to my mother late in life, was incapable of filling the traditional role of provider – some said through his own fault, while others blamed his bad luck. When this happened, Nuni did not stand by passively. She took over the provisioning of our household – from fruits, to the finest cuts of meat, to hearty desserts. Thanks to her, we ate exceedingly well. She never skimped. On the contrary, she made sure there was plenty of tasty food on the table. To this day, friends and relatives who had meals at our place remember the abundance of food and, in particular, the tender steaks that were served at lunchtime. She went daily to the grocery store, the meat man, the bakery, and the fruit and vegetable vendor. Some dishes she prepared herself; others were prepared by our household help under her supervision. She ate lunch with us every day and sometimes dinner too. My mother worked, came home for lunch, had a short nap, returned to work, came back home in the evening, had a light dinner with us and, more often than not, went out later in the evening. She never had to give a thought to our meals. The only times I remember her fretting about what would be served for lunch or dinner were when we had guests.

What feelings did Nuni and my mother have for each other? Nuni seemed genuinely fond of my mother – fond and admiring of her beauty and intelligence – and in turn, my mother admired Nuni's selflessness. But there were no real affinities between them. Nuni was twenty-three years older *than my mother, whose progressive views on a variety of subjects stood in sharp contrast to hers. This was not a source of conflict, my mother not being the sort who tried to hammer her views into anyone. Still, they belonged to different worlds, certainly in terms of how they lived their lives and the interests they had. I presume that they both felt indebted to one another: my mother, for obvious reasons; Nuni, for less obvious but equally powerful ones – for staying with my father, for maintaining a semblance of family life, and for making it easy for her to help. During my childhood years, I never once heard them exchange harsh words, never heard them say nasty things about each other in each other's absence. Nuni had plenty of ammunition against my mother; she could easily have alluded to my mother's liaisons but she never did, at least not in my presence. When, as a result of a particularly tense confrontation with my mother, my father moved in temporarily with her, Nuni continued to drop by our place loaded with fruits and assorted dishes, even though she would have lunch with him, at her place.*

Nuni and Gabrielle had far more in common than Nuni and my mother. They were both conventional though in a some-what different way. Perhaps their very conventionality stood in the way of a smooth relationship, for while Nuni's reference point was the extended family, Gabrielle put the marital bond above all else. Infinitely more freethinking than either, my mother could adjust to equivocal situations and accept unorthodox compromises. That made it easier for Nuni to get along with her than with Gabrielle.

When my father died, Nuni grieved with restraint. She was eighty years old then, had started to feel the weight of her age and would have been wondering how much longer she could continue providing our household with all she had been, how much longer she could keep going between her apartment and ours. Her two boarders were paying exceedingly low rents. Whatever little reserve she might have had would have been entirely used up by now. My father's death solved a problem that would have seemed insoluble to her: how to stop helping us, without seeming disloyal. Cruel as it may sound, his death was timely for her. She had reached the end of her resources – both financially and physically. At the funeral she barely cried. She visited us regularly after he died, probably twice a week, and never came empty-handed. She would bring us pastries, cheese puffs and bâtons salés, *handing us these treats apologetically, as if she ought to be giving us more. Sometimes, she would agree to stay for lunch. By then, our household consisted only of my mother and me – the rest of the family was scattered. My sisters and cousin were in Europe and Gabrielle traveled a lot. Nuni rarely talked about my father after he died.*

In addition to visiting us, she continued to visit the other branch of the family. These visits took place every Thursday, in the early evening when one of her cousins named Rosalie held tea receptions to which all family members were invited. Those tea receptions became an institution in the Conti family. Except during the period when the two branches of the family had had their famous quarrel, she attended virtually all of Rosalie's Thursdays. I sometimes went with her to these tea parties, divine occasions for a child with a sweet tooth. All the old aunts and uncles would heap sweets on my plate; I was the only child there. In between sweets, I would get whiffs of family gossip. And I got to know Joseph, Nuni's fiancé of long ago. By then in his early seventies, he would walk her back home. I could not imagine what Nuni had seen in him. I found him dull beyond belief. During their walks, he and Nuni would have animated conversations, mostly concerning family matters. Sometimes, the conversations turned into arguments. Once, he said something unflattering about my father, something to the effect that my father had behaved irresponsibly. I don't remember in what context. The remark made Nuni angry and, by the time we reached home, they were not speaking to one another. They made up the following Thursday. A good-natured woman, Rosalie made sure they did.

Family and love were the two subjects Nuni talked about at length – not only her love for her father, brothers and sister, but also romantic love; its nature, follies, mysteries. Yes, romantic love was very much on her mind. True love, she would say, rules out petty calculations and caution. There has to be a willingness to commit without holding anything back. You have to listen to the beat of your heart and to nothing else. Never try to figure out love. Never ask someone why she loves whom she loves, for 'love has its reasons which reason does not know.' When was the first time that Nuni hummed this line in my presence? I must have been really little since I cannot remember that first time. And did she use the word 'love', or the word 'heart'? Did she sometimes sing 'love has its reasons ...' and other times 'the heart has its reasons ...'? It is strange how I so vividly remember her humming that line while she stroked my hair or held my two hands in hers, swinging them sideways, left to right, then right to left, yet I cannot remember whether she sang 'love' or 'heart.'

One day, while we were discussing Joseph, Nuni said to me,

'You think I loved him: well, maybe I did, but the man I really loved was Aristote. Don't get funny ideas though; it was a platonic love, only platonic. Still, him I truly loved.' By then, I had already heard her use the term 'platonic love.' which she used frequently and had tried to explain to me, as much as it can be explained without spelling out what sexual love is about.

That was how she confessed to having loved Aristote, Bella's husband, a well-known surgeon and a pillar of Cairo's Greek community. Bit by bit, she would tell me more about that love of hers. The first time she fractured her femur, Aristote came to see her. She was in her fifties. He was in his forties; a big and handsome man, who liked to tell his patients to tough it out, be strong, forget about their aches and pains and, above all, to avoid medication. Nuni was small but tough and said no to surgery. He was impressed. She was immobilized at home for a few months – first in bed, then hobbling around that apartment, apparently holding on to a chair. I have no idea why a chair and not a cane. During those months that promised to be terribly tedious, a pattern developed. Aristote would drop by her place almost daily to check on her progress. She would have her household helper serve him his favorite dessert, milk pudding. As soon as she got better, she prepared the pudding herself. So he came by, ate the pudding, and they talked about one thing or another – always in Greek. That, in those circumstances, she would fall in love with the man is hardly surprising. And Aristote? It would be far-fetched to think that he came to view her in a sentimental light. She never claimed he had shown any sign of this. Still, I would like to think that he derived some pleasure from his visits. He was the kind of man who would have basked in a woman's quiet admiration. That *they talked in Greek would have constituted another draw for a man who valued all things Greek. For once then, the gods were kind to Nuni. What could have been a frustrating period in her life became a cherished period – one she would always associate with Aristote's visits. When she got better and started going out, his visits did not end altogether, though they became infrequent.*

When Nuni hummed 'love (or the heart) has its reasons which reason does not know,' did she have Aristote in mind? Was it because she had loved, in her fifties, a younger and successful man – a married man – whom she could never have expected to return her love?

Nuni is the one who taught me how to pull out a daisy's petals, one by one, saying, 'He loves me, he loves me not, he loves me ...' The first time we did this together, the flower said, 'He loves you' and I asked excitedly, 'But who is he, Nuni?' To which she replied, 'All the men who will count in your life'. I then asked, with false innocence, 'All the men? So there will be more than one?' Her answer was categorical: 'There will be only one you will truly love. As for all the others, you may believe for a little while you love them, but only one will remain locked in your heart forever.'

Every child should have a Nuni – the one grown-up who gives you treats every time you ask, who tells you family tales no one else would, who never scolds you, who makes you feel grown-up by talking to you about love. Yes, every child should have a Nuni, but Nunis deserve better than to be just Nunis, for the children will outgrow them and then what? My Nuni was buried, in my absence, in the Greek Orthodox cemetery in the Conti family crypt. There are two sides to the crypt – two sides for the two branches; the one that kept its money, and the branch that lost its money – her branch.

I realize that there is much I do not know about Nuni's life. I do not know how old she was when she got engaged; why her engagement was a very long one; whether she ever considered working; whether she knew sexual love.

Her engagement was problematic from the beginning, as it met with some opposition from Joseph's mother who did not get along with Nuni's mother and worried that her son might end up saddled with the financial mess likely to result from his cousins' extravagant habits. How much had Nuni herself wanted the marriage? She never said that the break-up broke her heart, but nothing can be inferred from this. She was too proud a woman to say such a thing. On a couple of occasions, she told me wistfully, 'He was very much in love with me once.'

As for work, when she was young, it would have seemed beneath her station, for what sort of work would have been available for a young woman in Cairo at the turn of the century? A lady's companion? A dressmaker? A milliner? A housekeeper? A governess? All these possibilities would have been ruled out. She was asked once whether she would consider working as a lady's companion but her brothers objected despite the prospect of her traveling to Europe on a luxurious boat. More acceptable activities would have included tutoring or teaching in schools. She had been a good student. I saw some of her school reports. I doubt though she ever seriously contemplated working when she was young. And when she got older, she was kept too busy by mother, sister and brothers to work.

Late in life she took boarders, a solution of last resort to her increasing financial problems. It had the advantage of being a discreet solution. Few people knew she had boarders, whom she came to regard as a necessary evil, treating them in an offhand fashion. They were single men of modest means and humble origins. They paid little and expected little. She made it obvious to them when they had encroached on her space. Yet she could be good to them, accepting deferred payment of their rent, advising them on family matters and listening to their sentimental woes. Often though, she set arbitrary rules concerning their use of the kitchen or bathroom or living room. Occasionally, she would threaten to evict them or raise their rent substantially, which she never did. The boarders were a constant reminder of the dramatic downturn in her family's fortune. No wonder she was sometimes gratuitously hard on these men. Except for her bedroom and theirs, she gradually stripped the apartment of furniture and knick-knacks so that, by the end of her life, it was virtually empty. She sold the furniture and knick-knacks because she needed the money.

I will not speculate on whether the pleasures of sexual love were known to her. I have no clues. She would have minded my speculating on this subject.

I have a hypothesis about Nuni and my father that may not apply to Helene and Nicolas, whom I never got to know. The hypothesis is that, both for Nuni and my father, money was a dirty subject and, for the longest time, they thought they were above money. The example of the other branch of the family so keen on making money would have reinforced those feelings. It could have worked very differently, driving them to do the same as opposed to the opposite and set themselves apart as they did. Setting themselves apart was more in keeping with their perception of themselves as superior – a perception they would have had from early on in their childhood, since they were the ones who had gone to the most exclusive schools, who had had friends in high circles, and who had grown up in the more elegant neighborhood. Thus, the image I have in mind is that of a close-knit extended family with two branches behaving like two children, each taking on a different role to establish their space and mark the difference. Fanciful? Perhaps, though plausible in a way.

Whatever the case may be, Nuni was a proud-hearted woman. I want to believe that she remained so till the end, but I do not know. I do not know whether it is possible to remain proud in poverty and loneliness. Of all the persons I have known, it strikes me that she was the most equipped to remain so in such circumstances.

1998: Gabrielle

Gabrielle came out of the car that dropped them off in front of the side entrance to the Ghezireh Sporting Club first, then Claire. They had been members since 1955, spending much of their leisure time there. To their daughters, the club had been a second home, the site of their first loves, where they could play any sport imaginable or just hang around.

The two elderly women headed towards 'the tea garden,' not arm in arm as many women their age do – Gabrielle abhorred that habit – nor even side by side. Ninety-year-old Gabrielle led the way.

Leaning on a cane, her eyes studying the pavement for bulges and potholes, Claire slowly followed. She was hoping that the friends they had arranged to meet would be on time. Her tête-à-têtes with Gabrielle tended to bring out a belligerence that was more contained in public than in private, although there were times when even the presence of third parties did not inhibit Gabrielle. A week earlier, at a supper organized by friends, Gabrielle had shown a frightening lack of self-restraint, spending much of the evening complaining about Claire, describing her as self-absorbed in the extreme, a bundle of absurd anxieties, senselessly medicating herself, and letting the household help get the better of her. All that had been said with such vitriol and an intensity so uncalled-for in a social gathering that Claire was mortified – not so much on her own account as on Gabrielle's for seeming on the verge of hysteria. For a moment, Claire had actually feared that Gabrielle would lose it. That Gabrielle's chronic irritability and touchiness could turn some day into something much worse, namely an uncontrollable fit, was an old and recurring fear of Claire's, brought on by Gabrielle having frequent outbursts hugely disproportionate to the apparent trigger.

Claire's presentiment at the time of Nicolas's death had come to pass: over the years, she had become a target of Gabrielle's generalized aggressiveness. And why should she have been spared when others, from their mother to Alexandre and Constance and even Nicolas, as well as assorted maids, cooks, tradesmen and drivers, had been the butt of it? Something about certain people seemed, however, to neutralize Gabrielle. That something seemed to be money and status. She never lashed out at a Yussef Sahli, or a George Conti, or her cousins Iris, Bella and brother John.

Her aggressiveness grew worse after Claire developed heart problems and came to depend on her. With all their daughters outside Egypt – Charlotte had stayed in Cairo for only six months back in 1978 – and the two of them living on the same floor in the same building, Claire found herself in the unenviable position of needing Gabrielle to accompany her to the doctor, help her organize the few bridge parties she still threw, pick up books for her from the French library, and put her car and driver at her disposal when finding a taxi was too daunting a prospect. All this Gabrielle did, though with bad grace.

But for her hearing, Gabrielle herself was in formidably good shape, still energetic, still keen on fashion, clothes and accessories, still unwilling to admit to any limitations of age. Hardly ever in need of a doctor, she seemed to take Claire's physical deterioration as a personal affront and the mark of a character deficiency. 'If only Claire could get a grip on herself' had become her refrain. This reaction to Claire's ailments was not unlike her reaction when her husband had fallen sick, except that she was yet more intolerant of Claire's condition as it reminded her of her own mortality. Claire's constant state of anxiety about her physical decline – besides her heart problems, she had a sore hip and almost continual ringing in one ear – incensed Gabrielle, who could not stand the manifestation of any vulnerability, physical or mental.

Whirling around her younger sister, concerned about her yet also exasperated by her, Gabrielle never missed a chance to contradict Claire. They were poles apart – in character, opinions and ways of dealing with people. So the subjects of disagreements between them abounded. Part of Gabrielle seemed bent on underscoring their differences, and part on hammering Claire into submission. Although a meek Claire would not have found favor with one who so valued strength of character, a quality she tended to equate with bossiness and saw therefore as sorely lacking in her sister.

Once, Gabrielle's daughter Aida, who was quite fond of her aunt, had asked her, 'But if Aunt Claire is as weak as you say she is, how do you explain Minya?' Gabrielle had dodged the question. Possessive in general, and of her daughter in particular, Gabrielle viewed with displeasure Aida's closeness to Claire. Aware of this, Claire and Aida avoided spending too much time together in her absence.

There were those in Claire's and Gabrielle's circle such as Iris and Bella who believed that at the root of Gabrielle's difficult character was pure and simple jealousy, her envious admiration of her sister. Not only had she been saddled with a younger sister endowed with intelligence and exceptionally good looks, but that sister also happened to be a more courageous sort. Despite her assertiveness, Gabrielle had always been less daring than Claire. At school, Claire had been the one willing to challenge authority, voice non-conformist views and confront physical challenges. Gabrielle was actually quite timid in some respects. It had taken her years to surmount her fear of water and learn to swim. Dozens of lessons, from the age of eight to the age of twelve, had not done it. Nicolas would eventually teach her, never managing, however, to have her put her face entirely in the water. Horse riding, a sport she would have loved to master, had proven too demanding, so nervous was she at the possibility of falling off. When she was seven and Claire six, their father had taken them on a desert excursion, then suggested a camel ride. 'Yes, yes,' the two girls had cried enthusiastically, yet, faced with the camel, Gabrielle's resolve would dissolve. Neither her father's entreaties nor the camel owner promising that the camel would walk – not even trot – had persuaded her to mount. She had burst into frenetic sobs, at the sight of which, despite desperately wanting to go for a ride, Claire had said that she too was afraid.

Claire recognized that a feeling of inferiority, all the harder to live with for a firstborn, and of which she was the unwitting cause, may have been behind Gabrielle's aggressive posture early on in life. Also, that the premature death of their father would have been particularly hard on Gabrielle, who was very close to him and saw herself as his favorite. His death had left her the odd one out in the triangle consisting of the mother and two daughters. What mystified Claire was why Gabrielle's aggressiveness should have persisted and in fact, intensified when, all in all, Gabrielle had done rather better with her life than she had. Claire considered that she now had more reasons to envy her sister than Gabrielle had reasons to envy her, if only because of Gabrielle's unrivaled good health. She was even coming to see some advantage in Gabrielle's ability to turn a blind eye to what she did not care to see, including any personal frailty or deficiency so, for example, Gabrielle had yet to concede that she spoke Arabic poorly. This self-deception, though not endearing, made her remarkably resilient in the face of old age: she talked as if it could have no effect on her. As for the long-term picture, Gabrielle's life had turned out rather better than one might have thought at the time of Nicolas's death. Sure, there had been major disappointments – a law degree leading nowhere and her daughter's divorce – as well as profound grief over the loss of Nicolas. But there had been a love story with a younger man that had brought her out of the austere and restless life into which she had sunk; then the loyal and enduring companionship of a devoted and long-suffering man who would have married her despite her harsh treatment of him; an unexpected boost to her financial affairs affording her a more than comfortable lifestyle; a post-retirement job that was ideal; and Egypt remaining, in her eyes, a desirable country in which to live.

'But watch your step! Your cane is more of a hindrance than a help,' Gabrielle shouted as she turned around and saw Claire about to stumble on a stone. 'I don't understand why you persist in using that cane. Get rid of it!'

'Without it, I feel lost.'

'It doesn't require much for you to feel lost,' Gabrielle said, then resumed walking. In recent weeks, she had been having problems with her eyesight, normally excellent, but was reluctant to tell Claire. She suspected that she might need a cataract operation and that frightened her, though she knew the intervention to be straightforward and painless.

In the tea garden, only a few tables were occupied. Their friends had not yet arrived. It was only 5:30 P.M. The garden would fill up later.

'Have you brought your shawl?' Gabrielle asked as they settled at a table. 'It will probably get cooler once the sun sets. That's how it typically is in September.'

'That's how it used to be. Now the summer heat seems to last forever.'

'I don't find it hot.'

'The temperatures have been around 33 all week long. That's hot to me.'

'You always find it hot.'

'Maybe so, but 33 degrees is not cool.'

'I said the temperatures would drop in the evening. I didn't say they were cool now, did I?'

To change the topic – it was potentially explosive as Gabrielle defended Cairo's weather the way one defends one's children – Claire observed that the recently married daughter of a friend of theirs did not seem quite as happy as one might expect. Mid-sentence, she realized that Gabrielle would likely see in her remark an indirect attack on marriage. She was right. Gabrielle immediately jumped to the defense of marriage, holding her responsible for their daughters' divorces – all four girls had divorced. By broadcasting her negative views on marriage, she had warped the girls' perspective, Gabrielle kept insisting. Claire defended herself, saying that she was not opposed to marriage, merely to staying in a bad one. Latching onto that statement, Gabrielle proceeded to dissect her sister's character, the gist of her indictment being that there was a huge chasm between what Claire professed and what she did, for hadn't she stayed in her marriage? So wasn't there an element of bad faith to the views she so casually put forth? Not bothering to point out that she held the views she did precisely because she had stayed in her marriage, Claire kept quiet, sensitive to the fact that Aida's divorce had been hugely upsetting to Gabrielle. But on the next subject they raised – how to treat maids – Claire would not keep quiet. Gabrielle's hard line annoyed her so much that Claire stated forcibly that it was none of Gabrielle's business whether she treated her household help with gloves so would Gabrielle stop interfering once and for all. Whenever Claire blew up at her sister, she regretted it afterwards. She was already regretting her little outburst when their friends arrived. The rest of the evening was peaceful. All focused on their friends, Gabrielle ignored Claire.

* * *

The next morning, Gabrielle let herself into Claire's apartment shortly after eight. She sometimes showed up that early to encourage Claire, who had a tendency to skip breakfast, to eat something. The reason she came early that morning was however to tell Claire about the arrest of dozens of fundamentalists, and the BBC coverage to which she listened whenever she managed to tune in on her short-wave radio. The two sisters were interested in politics. The one subject on which they saw eye to eye was Palestine: they were both sympathetic to the Palestinian cause. Their inability to read the Arabic papers made it hard for them to assess what was going on in the country, a subject on which they had, nevertheless, their opinions – differing opinions.

Claire was reading in bed. The shutters were closed. This would normally have invited some negative comment on Gabrielle's part. But her mind was on the news.

'Thank God for Mubarak,' Gabrielle said after announcing news of the arrests. 'One wouldn't have thought the man had as much muscle as he turned out to have. Muscle is exactly what is needed in the country.'

'With his security forces, he has the whole country under his thumb,' Claire said.

'Well, that's a good thing.'

'A good thing?'

'Sure! An excellent thing!' Gabrielle said. 'Too bad the world did not take his warnings seriously. He has been saying for years that terrorism is a huge problem.'

'Do we know for a fact that those arrested are terrorists? After all, he has been arresting Muslim Brothers, and others too. Are they all terrorists?'

Glaring at Claire, Gabrielle declared, 'I'm not about to shed tears for the arrest of Islamists. I wouldn't think you're a great sympathizer either.'

'Of course not,' Claire said. 'Still, I am not keen on seeing people go to jail, left and right.'

'Where does that leave you then?' Gabrielle asked loudly.

'Nowhere, I suppose.'

'You cannot deny that Egypt is infinitely more open under Mubarak than under Nasser, that people can breathe much more freely now! Would you rather live under a regime that is forced to resort to a certain amount of repression but still allows you to breathe, or under an Islamist-led regime?'

'You're spouting the government's line. Must it be one or the other? As long as the government restricts political freedoms, these are bound to be the only choices. You believe in a strong man. I don't.'

'You're your usual theoretical self. The reality is that Mubarak is containing elements you and I find undesirable. That's the reality. Yet you oppose him. Where's the logic? I am a realist and I find it extremely annoying to hear the sort of argument you're making. In fact, I don't see any real argument in what you're saying.'

'You asked me what I think. I told you what I think, but you don't like it. I cannot help it if I happen to have a different opinion from yours.' With a tone that seemed both dispirited and impatient, Claire went on, 'What do I know anyway about the country's political ins and outs? What do we know?'

'What do you mean?'

'I mean we're so out of touch that it's difficult for us to have a meaningful opinion.'

'Speak for yourself. I don't see why we cannot have meaningful opinions. We're from the country, were born here, have lived here all of our lives. I certainly feel entitled to my opinions on the country's political situation. I'm perfectly capable of forming an opinion.'

'It's good you feel that way. I wish I did, but I don't.'

'Spare me *that*, please. Don't start saying we don't belong.'

'Look, I'm speaking for myself. You cannot tell me what to feel, or what not to feel. I'm not questioning the way you feel, or telling you how you ought to feel! But how can we pretend we're informed when we don't read the Arabic papers and only read the pathetic French dailies intended for people like us?'

'Your problem is that you complicate everything and end up

making your life much more difficult than it could be. Both for you and also for those around you, need I point out.'

'Shall we just talk about politics and not talk about me?'

Shrugging, Gabrielle said, 'I can tell you that I certainly hope Mubarak's son succeeds his father. He's apparently unpretentious, sociable, and smart. My dentist's granddaughter was at university with him. In the same faculty. She knows him.'

'It's no surprise that somebody from the American University in Cairo views him favorably but what about the rest of the country, the vast majority? Besides, will the army and the security forces back him?'

'Charlotte was going to go to AUC, so what do you have against the AUC crowd?'

'Nothing at all. But it is ultra-privileged, it does not reflect public opinion.'

'You seem to think that the army would oppose Mubarak's son. I don't think so. They certainly don't want the Islamists to take over.'

'I would not be so sure of that. Hamid Hassanein was telling me the other day that many in the army sympathize with them.'

'Anything Hamid Hassanein tells you, you believe.'

'He's well-informed and measured.'

'Measured?'

'Yes, measured!'

'But he's on the left!'

'So what? Despite his political convictions, he has been part of a team of human rights lawyers defending Muslim Brothers.'

'You had not told me that you're in touch with him. What for?'

'The same thing, the same thing,' Claire muttered.

'You mean the apartment?'

'Yes, yes. I would like the girls to keep it after I die. At least, to have that option.'

'You're hard to fathom. One minute you're all doom and gloom about Egypt, in which case why should the girls want to keep the apartment? The next minute you're tormenting yourself about what will happen to the apartment in case you die.'

'There's no "in case," Gabrielle, death is not a likelihood. It will come, sooner for me I hope than later. And I'm not being inconsistent. My preferences may not reflect the girls' preferences. They may want to spend time in Egypt at some point.'

'They show no sign of it.'

'People change. Circumstances change too. After all, Charlotte toyed with the idea of coming back.'

'That was years ago.'

'Gabrielle, why are you finding it so hard to understand my desire to leave them the apartment? Why? It seems to me that it's a normal desire. It seems to me that it would be strange if I didn't try.'

'And what did Hamid Hassanein have to say on the subject?' Gabrielle asked belligerently. 'I doubt very much there's a chance they could inherit it. They don't live here. The law clearly gives a building's owner the right to take the apartment back.'

'You're right, unfortunately. Unless one fudges and pretends the girls live here, which is not an easy thing to do.'

'You could have asked me, there was no need to see your lawyer for that.'

'I don't doubt your legal reasoning abilities, but the laws have changed a great deal and keep changing. So I keep hoping.'

'For being as intelligent as you are, you sometimes lack common sense. The changes have all been in the landlords' favor.'

'But tell me, why are you so critical of my attempts at finding some way to leave the apartment to the girls?'

'You're worrying too much about it, and it's a morbid subject. Quite morbid.' Gabrielle got up and proceeded to open the shutters, saying, 'I really don't understand how you can live in this penumbra. Don't you feel the need for light and fresh air? The first thing I do in the morning, even before I make my coffee, is to open the windows for some fresh air.'

'Fresh air? Can't you smell the pollution?'

'Oh, just a tiny bit of a burning smell.'

'Surely, more than a bit. Much more than a bit. They have been talking about it even in the papers.'

'It's one more thing the critics of the regime have jumped on to discredit it. It's not the government's fault if the farmers burn rice, and if people choose to burn their garbage.'

'It would be better for the government to focus on that problem than on arresting people indiscriminately.'

'I disagree. The fight against terrorism should be the priority. The Hatchepsut massacre just about wiped out tourism.'

'Would you please close at least one of the windows? I find the honking and the noise unbearable.'

'But it's no different than on any other day.'

'Well, today I cannot stand it. Perhaps because the ringing in my ears is worse than usual.'

'Call your doctor!' Gabrielle said as she half-closed one window. 'Why isn't Zeinab here? It's past 8:30. When she used to work for me, I insisted she arrive before 8:15, and she did. I can assure you.'

'She was younger then. Besides, she told me she would be a bit late.'

'As I said yesterday, you need to be firmer with her and also with Azza. You give them too much leeway.'

'I need them.'

'So?'

'It's no sinecure to be looking after me as you can attest to.'

'They're paid for it. And if you include all the tips the girls give them when they visit, they're very well paid. More so than most. Do you know what the going market rate is?'

'No, no, and I don't want to know,' Claire said. 'The way prices have been going, whatever they get is peanuts. Judging by my own financial situation, I wonder how they're managing. I put myself in their shoes. They're getting on in age. It cannot be easy for them to keep working. They have their own health problems.'

'Zeinab's biggest problem is her useless husband. He's twenty years younger than her and cannot stick to a job. She's probably out and about trying to find him one. Now she's an energetic woman. She won't let herself be defeated. She confronts what needs to be confronted head on. I admire that in her. That's why we got along.'

'You quarreled, all the time,' Claire was about to remind Gabrielle but merely said, 'She's energetic, but she's in her late sixties, and so is Azza.'

'I was very fit in my sixties. You were in pretty good shape too. And remember Constance, all the walking she used to do, up into her seventies? Azza is a big complainer.'

'Azza may be a complainer, but have you seen her knees, how swollen they get?'

'Why don't you have Dr. Ramzi look at them?'

'I did. It's arthritis.'

'Exercise is what she needs. She's far better off working than staying at home. Her children drive her crazy and exploit her.'

Still standing, Gabrielle said in a cryptic way, 'Well, I have several things to do this morning. I must be going.'

Claire did not ask her sister what she had to do. Gabrielle was secretive about both the small and big things in her life.

'Thanks for dropping by,' Claire said.

'I'll pick you up at five o'clock. We're expected at the club at 5:30.'

'Don't count on me.'

'Why?'

'I'm not feeling up to it.'

'You have the whole day to rest. How can you prejudge how you'll be feeling? Staying at home all day long can do you no good.'

'We'll see, but, as I said, don't count on my coming.'

'You're being difficult,' Gabrielle said before leaving in a huff.

'At least it did not degenerate into a quarrel,' Claire told herself. 'How she does not see that she kills any pleasure I would derive from her company is beyond me. How can she be so insensitive? I would have gladly gone to the club, but I cannot bear the thought of more friction.'

* * *

Later that morning, when told of the car accident in which Gabrielle had died on the spot even though Osta Ramadan, her driver, was barely hurt, Claire was at first incredulous.

She was in the midst of sorting old bills when the doorbell rang. Zeinab went to see who it was and returned all flustered to say that two men and a shaken Osta Ramadan were at the door.

'Turn left, *left* I say!' Gabrielle had apparently screamed at him. Rattled, he had not seen the oncoming truck running a red light.

That was Osta Ramadan's version – a plausible version considering Gabrielle's urge to control his driving, his tendency to ignore her instructions, and Cairo's frenzied traffic.

'But where were you going?' Claire asked him.

'You won't believe it,' he said while dabbing his eyes, 'to the cemetery. Yes, the cemetery. *Sitt* Gabrielle – may the Almighty Lord be good to her – had ordered repairs to be done to the family vault and wanted to check on the work.'

'The family vault?'

'Yes, her husband's. Hadn't she told you? To fix the damage it sustained after the earthquake.'

'At least, she did not suffer. Rest assured, she did not,' one of the two gentlemen told Claire. A doctor, who happened to be present at the scene of the accident, he had felt compelled to accompany Osta Ramadan back to the apartment. The other gentleman was a security man, one of the many keeping an eye on Cairo's streets.

Claire walked to her bedroom, sat on her bed and looked at the windows with their closed shutters. It occurred to her then that she was free, completely free to do as she pleased, at the age of eighty-eight. That was when the tears began trickling down her face.

'What's a life?' Claire Sahli wondered. The answer seemed obvious to her: 'if you're young, it's the future; not so young, it's the present; old, it's the past; and very old, it's the deaths of all those who mattered in your life.' As she now saw it, that's what a life seemed to be. A succession of deaths, one after the other.

Zeinab came in and sat next to her. Zeinab sitting close to her on the bed reminded Claire of the day, seventy-five years earlier, when she and Gabrielle had sat next to one another, mourning their father in quiet harmony. A major sense of failure, more profound even than when Alexandre died, overcame her.

More than any other deaths in her life, Gabrielle's death would make Claire reflect on the inexplicable nature of love. Despite everything, she had loved Gabrielle, but she was not so sure that Gabrielle, caught up in proving to herself and the world that they were different, had loved her. Would it have made a difference had she been more demonstrative of her affection for Gabrielle? Might this have disarmed her sister? That the two of them had not got along better was such a terrible waste, Claire kept thinking as the tears continued to trickle down her face.

The one and only time Gabrielle had raised the subject of her death, it was to say, in Claire's and Aida's presence, that she wanted to be buried with her husband, in the Conti vault. She, Claire, wanted to be buried in the Sahli vault, where her mother and father were buried. The two sisters' separateness in death would thus bear out their emotional separateness in life.

Claire's three daughters came to attend Gabrielle's funeral and left with promises to return soon. Simone, a simultaneous interpreter and on her own – her children were grown up – was between jobs and about to move to New York. Djenane, partnered both in work and in life with a professional mime, was scheduled to perform in a festival in Germany; she had no children and used as a *pied-à-terre* a small house in the south of France. Charlotte, whose children attended university in Montreal, divided her time between Montreal and and Morocco where she was doing anthropological work.

During their short stay in Cairo – a mere few days – the three girls had convinced Claire to hire help round the clock. Both Zeinab and Azza were willing to work longer hours and offering to find additional help, if needed. Gabrielle's car was apparently salvageable so, with Aida's accord, Claire's daughters decided to keep it as well as keep Osta Ramadan on a part-time basis, their joint present to their mother.

There had been no mention of Claire moving in with any one of them. She had not expected them to offer. The very last thing she wanted was to saddle them with her infirmities and re-enact her mother's last years. The thought of becoming dependent on them was intolerable to her. She was determined to spare them having to look after her, even if that meant going into a home. On days when her need of Gabrielle had weighed heavily upon her, she had entertained the thought of moving into a home, only to defer acting upon it in the hope that death would intervene.

Was Claire, nevertheless, hurt that her daughters had not offered to take her in? There was a flicker of sadness but no more than a flicker. Her daughters' well-being mattered more to her than the relationship they had with her. Once, in a discussion with Gabrielle, she had said she could understand a mother cutting off all ties with her child, if that were necessary for the child's happiness. She thought herself quite capable of doing just that. Gabrielle had said she did not believe a word of it.

* * *

After Gabrielle's death, Aida stayed in Cairo for a month during which Claire saw her every day. Unhappy in her third marriage, Aida was consumed with guilt towards her mother for having had a series of unsuccessful unions when Gabrielle had valued marital stability above all else. 'I caused her upset needlessly,' she confided in Claire. 'I might as well have stayed with my first husband. How could I have made such a series of mistakes?' Claire believed there was a simple answer, namely, that making a major mistake in life tended to put one on the wrong track. As far as Claire was concerned, the idea that one learnt from one's mistakes was more myth than reality. She said so to Aida, with whom she felt she could speak without censoring herself. With her daughters, she had to be more careful.

Aida left and the days seemed never-ending despite the occasional outing, frequent phone calls from friends and regular visits from the most faithful amongst them. Though she wanted them, she sometimes turned down those visits when making the effort to look presentable and show interest in other people's lives seemed both colossal and futile. The one visit she always looked forward to was that of a friend who brought her books and articles, the wife of a man much enamored of Claire years earlier and now dead. The wife had known of his infatuation but never held it against Claire. She had had her own dalliances.

On Sunday mornings, Iris called her from Geneva. Greatly diminished physically, Iris remained as fond of Claire as she had been when she was twenty and Claire thirty, the summer they had spent together in Alexandria bicycling and reading Proust on the beach at Sidi Bishr. The line at the end of the first chapter of *The Fugitive* that reads '... but thought tires and memory decays' had made Iris exclaim one evening, her cheeks ablaze, 'Oh, to die before that happens.'

Iris's memory had not decayed. From Proust, Camus, Kant, Rimbaud, Baudelaire, she could still quote entire passages. Her heart, though, had hardened. She had come to view her siblings with mistrust, feeling that they had given her much less than they had got from her. Anger at her father for having loved her badly – if at all – overflowed since the death of her husband. In her affection for Claire, she remained constant, calling her every Sunday morning before going to church. Malcontent, Iris had turned to religion – a subject she and Claire avoided discussing. She called Claire even when she felt unusually low or bitter, which happened more and more often. When they were young and she was upset about something, she used to want Claire to appease her. Now she wanted Claire to espouse her views and sanction her anger. That Claire resisted playing that role did not seem to put her off, as Claire took her seriously.

To Claire, Zeinab and Azza had become indispensable. Not just for the services they rendered but also for their mere presence. Whenever she was on her own in the apartment – usually between their two shifts – her anxiety bubbled to the surface and would only abate once she heard a key clicking in the entrance door to the apartment, announcing the arrival of either one of them. She would hear the click because she waited for them in the entrance room. She did not quite understand why she was so anxious. She did not think she feared death. But why then was she fretting every day about medication, about finding the right doctor or the right physiotherapist? 'Because I don't want to suffer,' was the only answer she could think of. 'Yes to death, but no to pain and suffering. That's why.' Still, that answer did not explain her profound unease at being left alone in the apartment, her need for a presence, silent or lively. Living had become a tedious exercise in survival that made little sense, and yet she kept at it, albeit without zest.

Sometimes Zeinab, not one for mincing her words, would tell her, 'You cannot count on children nowadays. That's why I had none. Trust me, you're much better off here, mistress of your own affairs than in their care, however well-intentioned they may be.'

Azza, on the other hand, kept wondering if Charlotte might

at some point think of coming to Egypt for an extended period. 'Couldn't she do some of her work here?' she often asked Claire.

Zeinab and Azza had radically different temperaments which was a good thing, for when Claire grew tired of one, the other would arrive and the atmosphere change. Married four times, Zeinab was capable, assertive, never at a loss for words or an answer and endowed with a strength belied by her tiny but muscular build. She loved doing errands, supervising tradesmen, and would much rather move furniture and polish wooden floors than cook. Azza was big and timid. She was married to a man who had taken a second wife. Deeply hurt, she had nevertheless accepted that second marriage as being part of the fate she had to endure. Baking pastries was what she did best. Claire much admired that skill, having tried her hand at baking pastries late in life and found it a challenging task. It upset Azza that Claire no longer enjoyed baking, though they still discussed recipes.

Every now and then, thoughts of suicide would go through Claire's mind, but in an abstract way. She knew that she lacked the courage needed for that. Never before had she toyed with the idea of suicide, neither after ending her affair with Guy, nor in her grief over the death of little Yves.

She still read, though with less pleasure. Over the years, she had jotted down her opinion of the books she read: 'excellent, very good, good, mediocre, poor.' In recent months, there had been fewer ticks in the columns reserved for 'excellent' and 'very good' books. She did not know whether to attribute this to the fact that she was no longer choosing her own books, or to her sinking morale.

Of Gabrielle she thought a great deal, every time returning to the same question, 'Why did it have to be the way it was between us?'

Four months after Aida had left, Zeinab died in her sleep. Zeinab's much younger husband came one morning in tears to give the news to Claire. She was stunned. First Gabrielle, now Zeinab, when she – not Zeinab – was the one with a weak heart. 'My sister will fill in for her,' the husband offered between sobs. He seemed profoundly shaken. Claire was moved to see him so shaken. 'I liked Zeinab a lot,' she told him, meaning it. 'I lost a lot by losing her,' he said, shaking his head. 'People didn't understand why I married her as she was much older than me. They all thought I was after her money and her little plot of land near the Pyramids. But they were wrong. I loved her.' After he had calmed down, he sat in the kitchen, staring at the floor.

Azza made him a cup of tea. She was the one crying now. Claire too sat in the kitchen. 'I also lost a lot by losing her,' she told Zeinab's husband. Moving into a home was probably unavoidable now.

* * *

Two days later, an unexpected offer from Aida, unrelated to Zeinab's death, would throw Claire into a state of great confusion.

'I left Max,' Aida told Claire over the phone. 'It could not go on. I realized this after Mother's death. It took me some time to gather the courage to do it. He has moved out. Aunt Claire, we're alone, you and I. We get along, we always have. I think you should come and live with me in Paris. I need you.' Aida had not heard yet about Zeinab's death. Anticipating Claire's objections, she hurried to add, 'You'll tell me you don't have the strength for such a big move but Paris is not so far from Cairo. The apartment is big. You'll have your own room and bathroom. There's no reason for you to live in Cairo on your own and for me to be in this big apartment on my own. Besides, you love Paris. Whenever you visited, you seemed to feel quite at home.'

'Aida, you'll get over your break-up with Max. You two might get back together and, even if you don't, you'll remake your life.'

'No, I won't,' Aida interjected. 'I won't live again with a man.'

'This mood of yours will pass. Still, it's enormously kind of you to invite me to come live with you, even if it's unrealistic. I would not be easy to live with – not at my age and in my condition. Gabrielle had reasons to get irritated with me. It's not as if I am not aware of this. Yes, I love Paris, but Paris at my age?'

'Please, think about it. I'm serious. It makes absolute sense for us to be joining forces.'

'Except there are no forces on my side, darling.'

'Aunt Claire, you're remarkably fit, perhaps not physically but in all other ways. The children would love you to come to Paris, particularly Vincent who talks about you often. I'm sure I'll get to see much more of them, if you come. So your presence would benefit me in more than one way.'

'Poor Zeinab died,' Claire said.

'Oh no! How? When?' Aida asked.

'Just two days ago. In her sleep. The death I wish upon myself. I was about to call you to tell you.'

'It grieves me very much,' Aida burst out. Then, after a few silent seconds, she said, 'Remember how she used to try to mediate between Mother and me. She was quite something. She wasn't in the least afraid of Mother. She could scream as loud as her and did! They were both so energetic. They both seemed eternal.'

'She was in her sixties – late sixties probably. Her death has affected me more than I would have thought and not only because of the loss of her services. I liked her.'

'How are you managing without her?'

'Her husband sent me his sister the very afternoon he came to tell me the news.'

'Are you satisfied with his sister?'

'So-so. But I'm not in a position to be fussy. I get the feeling she's trustworthy enough. She must be in her forties. Her name is Abla. Azza does not seem to mind her, and that's important.'

'Aunt Claire, do think of coming here. It's not an impulsive offer. Believe me.' Aida hesitated before saying, 'It should not pose a problem as far as Simone, Djenane and Charlotte are concerned. Their lives are less settled than mine,' and, with the hint of a laugh, she specified, 'geographically, I mean.'

Claire did not doubt Aida's sincerity and knew her to be the sort of person to live up to her commitments, but she could not imagine foisting herself on Aida in her current condition. That they had perhaps more in common than Claire had with her own daughters was not enough for her to feel comfortable at the thought of Aida looking after her in her dying days, which was what it would amount to. It was less frightening a prospect than that of imposing that burden on any one of her daughters – in Aida's case there would be at least an element of free will. Still, she could not put herself and Aida in that situation.

And yet, after their telephone conversation, she thought about the offer all the time. It was on her mind from the minute she woke up to when she went to bed, including when she tried to read. It even kept her awake some nights. It put her in the same tortured state of mind into which she had sunk, some thirty years earlier in Beirut, except that this time her being so tormented made no sense whatsoever. It was totally out of proportion with the objective situation since she had already decided that the offer was not viable, however tempting it was.

Every day, she would go through the pros and cons of leaving Cairo to go and live with Aida in Paris, as if it were a choice she was actually considering. Telling herself that it was pure madness for her to be obsessing about a choice she had already ruled out did not have the desired calming effect. She came close to begrudging Aida her offer.

One morning, studying her reflection in the bathroom mirror, Claire said to herself resolutely, 'Looking at that face should be sufficient to disabuse me of any crazy notion of going anywhere. Here I'll stay till the end.'

The mirror recipe did not work. Claire continued to let the lure of Paris torture her. Gabrielle was often on her mind during those days and nights – a Gabrielle resentful of the idea of her moving in with Aida. She felt disloyal towards her sister for contemplating that idea, even in hypothetical terms.

One night, kept yet again awake by thoughts of Paris, she considered the matter from an angle that helped her put the idea out of her mind: she could not accept Aida's offer because of her daughters. Even if she were up to the move, she would have to turn it down on their account. While her moving into a home might cause them some guilt, her being looked after by their cousin risked causing them a greater measure of it. They would be put in an awkward situation – a situation that would give them reasons to feel displaced in her affection for them and also remiss. She did not want that.

After that night, Claire's agitation over Aida's offer gradually subsided. She never once mentioned the offer to her daughters and asked Aida to do the same.

Claire's Paris fantasy – as she would later refer to it – gave way to internal turmoil brought on by the question of whether to move into a home, or to gamble on being fit enough till the end to continue living in her apartment. That was not a speculative question. It too would give her sleepless nights, although, curiously, the Paris fantasy had been more agonizing. This made her wonder whether it was easier to resign oneself to the prospect of definite unhappiness than to some happiness almost but not quite within reach.

Epilogue

In the weeks leading to her death – there was no obvious sign of its imminence but for a strong feeling on her part that it was nearing – one thought, a question really, would take hold of Claire: if she was still lucid just before the very end, what would she be thinking of; who would be on her mind? Would she be trying to take stock of what this life of hers had amounted to? Would she have some last-minute illuminating insight? Or would she feel regret for the way she had dealt with the hand that was given her? Would she be thinking of those dear to her she was about to leave, or of those who had already left? Or of lines she had read and which had stayed with her, such as: 'Love is not an inevitable part of life, it is only a circumstance, a crisis ... a terrible crisis ... it passes, and that's all?' or, 'I like independence in everything.' Might that be her last thought, she who had felt so constrained all along?

At the intensive-care unit of the hospital to which Claire was admitted after suffering heart failure, her daughters and Aida walk in and out of the room where Claire is hooked to tubes and machines, her heart still beating, thanks to the doctors' efforts to keep her alive until her daughters' arrival – all three of them. The doctors have succeeded, though Claire may have had something to do with it. The nurses are convinced she hung in there to get to see her daughters one last time, after which, in all likelihood, she will let go.

Because of the tubes, Claire cannot speak, but she can understand what is being said to her and, with her head and hand as well as through her eyes, she is able to respond.

When Charlotte asks her how she is feeling, her eyes say, 'What sort of question is this? Cannot you see for yourself?' But her hand gestures 'so-so' as her own ineptness when Uncle Yussef was dying – her mentioning celebrating his birthday – comes back to her.

For a brief moment she is alone with Aida and immediately grabs the opportunity to tell her – one hand serving as her voice – to disconnect her from the tubes and the machines. 'Cut, cut, cut,' says her hand. The intended meaning is unmistakable. 'Cut, cut, cut,' she gestures again with a pleading expression. The color draining from her already tired face, Aida takes Claire's hand, the one that says, 'Cut, cut, cut,' and, with a voice meant to provide comfort and convey conviction, she says, 'But Aunt Claire, you're over the worst, you'll improve, you'll see. You have already improved.' Claire frowns.

Half an hour later, alone with Djenane, Claire repeats the 'Cut, cut, cut' gesture – this time her expression is resolute. All that Djenane can think of saying is, 'But Mother, what are you asking me to do? Be reasonable. The doctor will be coming any time now.' Claire turns her face away from her daughter and closes her eyes. She keeps them shut while Djenane talks at random, hoping to keep her mother interested in life. She keeps them shut when, later, each one of her daughters and Aida give her a kiss, saying that they are going to their hotel to rest and will be back in a couple of hours. It is just after dawn when they leave. It happens to be Election Day. The Muslim Brothers, running as independents, are expected to do well.

Twenty minutes later Claire's ninety-six-year-old heart stops beating. The doctors on duty, alerted by beeping machines, decide to do nothing. Over the course of the night, they have seen Claire's three daughters and niece stream in and out of her room.

Glossary

ahwa coffee shop.

al-Azhar the oldest institution of higher learning in the Muslim world.

bac (baccalauréat) French high school diploma.

bâtons salés salted snacks.

bawab doorman.

Bey Turkish official rank below that of Pasha, and like it, also used in an honorific sense, even after both titles were abolished in 1952.

Cicurel a department store.

Darb al-Geneina (Alley of the Garden), a neighborhood created in the nineteenth century below the citadel for the elite and the functionaries of the Khedive (the title of the viceroy of Egypt from 1867 to 1914).

Dinshawai village in the Delta close to which on June 13, 1906, a pigeon-shooting outing by British officers resulted in a fracas between the officers and the villagers.

Free Officers the group of officers who engineered the 1952 *coup d'état* and overthrew King Faruq.

galabeyah	ample robe-like outer garment.
Greenshirts	paramilitary organization modeled on fascist youth leagues. Activist wing of the Young Egypt party (Misr al-Fatat).
hallawa	halva; sweet made of sesame.
higab	head covering.
Ikhwan	(Brothers). The term refers to the society of Muslim Brothers founded in 1928.
Ismailiya	a city on the Suez Canal founded in 1861 under Khedive Ismail as a depot for the canal excavation.
Khawaga	term used colloquially to refer to or address westerners and members of Egypt's foreign minorities.
Maglis al-Umma	National Assembly.
Mazmazel	Egyptian pronunciation of the French word 'mademoiselle.'
mehalabeyah	milk pudding.
melayah	black sheet of cloth in which mainly working-class women wrap themselves when they go out.
midan	square.
Midan Ismailiya	square in the heart of downtown Cairo named after Khedive Ismail under whose rule it was laid out. The square was renamed Midan al-Tahrir (Liberation Square) after the coup of July 1952.
Mufatescha	Inspector.
Om	mother.
Osta	'Master.' The term is often used with reference to a cook or the master of a craft or a trade as well as to address or refer to, respectfully, older men without much formal education.

Rivos Egyptian brand of aspirins.

Sayidah Zeinab Working- and lower middle-class district of Cairo.

Sirdar Persian title brought to Egypt by the British to denote the commander-in-chief of the Anglo-Egyptian army.

Sitt Mrs.; Madam; lady.

suffragi butler.

'ud string musical instrument.

Ustaz Mr.

Wafd (Delegation). A delegation formed at the close of World War I to present the case for Egypt's independence to the British government and the Versailles Peace Conference. It was organized as a parliamentary party in 1924.